Mostly on *Sunday*

Sarah Johnston

ISBN 978-1-64670-426-2 (Paperback)
ISBN 978-1-64670-427-9 (Hardcover)
ISBN 978-1-64670-428-6 (Digital)

Copyright © 2020 Sarah Johnston
All rights reserved
First Edition

All rights reserved. No part of this publication may be reproduced, distributed, or transmitted in any form or by any means, including photocopying, recording, or other electronic or mechanical methods without the prior written permission of the publisher. For permission requests, solicit the publisher via the address below.

Covenant Books, Inc.
11661 Hwy 707
Murrells Inlet, SC 29576
www.covenantbooks.com

Prologue

In Central Pennsylvania's Allegheny Appalachians, there are two neighboring valleys nestled snugly in the arms of the watery tributaries that drain into the west branch of the Susquehanna River. These valleys lay claim to fertile farmland, timber, coal, natural gas resources, and cool sweet soft water. And these fertile valleys support the growth of the sweetest peaches in the world. When the immigrants got off the boat in Philadelphia, they were headed for the great west with promises of land, gold, and opportunity. But after a few days' journey, some wagon trains stopped here, probably for an overnight, to give Mama time to cook supper and wash out the baby's diapers. During this respite, they found the cool streams cascading to the Susquehanna River and the soil so dark and rich that it did not seem necessary to go any further. In particular, the Germans, Welsh, and Eastern Europeans decided that there was enough similarity to their homelands that they could prosper and thrive in this environment. The Germans and the Welsh settled in the West Valley which was cradled in the arms of two mountain ranges, Crescent Ridge to the northwest and Coal Hill to the southeast. The Eastern Europeans settled in the East Valley, just several miles east of Coal Hill.

At first, these three cultures did not believe that they had much in common, so they built their own communities with separate one-room schoolhouses and little churches. And some of those enclaves did survive for many years, independent and reclusive; but as the school systems had to consolidate in order to thrive and keep up with the times, the children made friends and moved the culture into the modern era and—heaven forbid—even intermarried. It was natural that this trisect was going to happen; it was just a matter of time. But even now, it is possible to journey onto the back roads and find some small enclaves still clinging to the old ways, keeping their culture pure. The valleys were rich in folklore, home remedies, soothsayers, fortune tellers, and tea-leaf readers.

For some people, it is the seashore, and for others, simply a large rock thrown up out of the earth in some prehistoric cataclysmic upheaval. For Henry David Thoreau, it was a small pond carved out of the earth by glacial retreat. Thoreau tells us why he went to his pond, "I did not wish to live what was not life." In other words, he did not want to discover that he had not lived after it was too late. For the people in West Valley, a hike up to Crescent Ridge provided a special place whenever major decisions were to be made. The highest peak on Crescent Ridge, overlooking the West Valley, was nicknamed Caleb's Lookout and later shortened to just Caleb's. If one squinted real hard or used binoculars, one could get a tiny peek across Coal Hill into East Valley.

Lila, from the West Valley, was familiar with the hike to the lookout since she was born unto this place and taken there by her parents who were taken there by their parents. On Sundays, it was okay to skip church if you were reverently hiking up to Caleb's. From up there, you could look down into West Valley and beyond where your mind could see forever with 20-20 vision. Unlike Thoreau, you do not have to remain up there for two years, two months, and two days to figure out what life should mean to you. On cloud wings, transcendental thought wafted across the sky in waves of clarity. It didn't matter to Lila whether she was searching for God or for her inner child; as far as she was concerned, it was all one stretched-out continuum.

When Lila thought about her early childhood, she realized that she was born just at the tail end of the Great Depression, only then to be raised during the WWII. This back-to-back calamitous duo produced some very hearty individuals, such as her parents who saved every scrap of string wrapped around a paper ball and every piece of tinfoil crinkled into the war effort. There was pressure on everyone to tighten your belt, pick yourself up by the bootstraps, and make something out of almost nothing. Also most of the children felt the unspoken pressure to do better in their schoolwork. Probably due to both nurture and nature, Lila felt all of this quite keenly. And any idea that she has now as an adult still has to wend its way up through her inner child, slightly deflected by subsequent life events before it sees the light of day. Whenever Lila journeyed up to Caleb's, she could figure out which childhood impressions she should jettison and which ones she wanted to keep as her mantle. Show me the child and I will show you the adult.

Several years ago, Lila's life was at a standstill and stagnant. She had done all the right things, majored in biochemistry in college, met and married a great guy, and had an interesting job at a chemical plant which manufactured designer chemicals for the pharmaceutical industry. However, life sometimes gets in the way, and this was clearly happening now to Lila. At middle age, her husband had died of congestive heart failure—they were never able to have children; and as a lot of women experienced in the 1960s and 1970s, there was a ceiling preventing advancement. And sometimes, they had a to carry an inordinate amount of the mundane work necessary around any workplace.

Lila decided that it was time to go back to her ancestral home and take a restorative hike up to Crescent Ridge where she thought through her options. She could keep plugging on at the chemical plant or she could come back home and restart the chicken and bee farm. She had inherited the cottage and land; both parents were gone. She knew that some people said that you could not go home again, and Gertrude Stein wrote, "There is no there, there." *Well, maybe*, thought Lila, *some people don't know in which "there" to look.*

She came away from the mountain ridge thinking that she could take an unpaid sabbatical from the chemical plant, with a consultant status to maintain her ties, just in case she did want to go back after the leave. The plant agreed to pay her a small stipend for her consultant status. She did restart the bee and chicken farm, made many improvements on the cottage, got a dog named Benny, made some new friends, and communicated with some old friends, especially Violet, a childhood friend. After years of separation, Lila convinced Violet to come back to the valley for a weeklong reunion; there were many questions she wanted to ask her about unusual and mysterious events that happened here years ago. They were an unlikely pair, both born in the West Valley but into very different cultures and lifestyles. However, at a very young age and quite by accident, they discovered that they could communicate without the spoken word; this knowledge formed a tight-knit lifelong bond. Anxiously now, Lila is preparing for the visit.

Getting Ready for the Visit

Day 1: Monday

Over morning coffee on the patio, Lila reflected on the early years when the Stanton family provided much of the entertainment and much of the gossip in these parts, especially for Blind Elsie who listened in on her party line. Elsie was on the same party line as the Stanton's, so she knew much of their personal history, at least all that was fit to be whispered over the telephone lines. Everyone knew that this was Elsie's window to the world, and it was just accepted as a minor nuisance. Elsie was always first to know who was scheduling a "seeing" with Madame Holly Stanton. In those days, if you had need of absolute privacy, you hand-delivered your own message. Dropping it in the mailbox was almost as bad as a phone call because Baufman, the mail carrier, was also a bit of a snoop.

Sitting there in the sunshine, Lila was recalling her first seeing experience and remembered that she was not quite thirteen when she and cousin Bonnie, already thirteen, believed they were worldly and sophisticated. After all, they were taken by Aunt Sue to piano lessons, shopping in Alma, and occasional grown-up picture shows at the Ritz. Furthermore, they were often invited to a friend's house to watch television, a little grainy, but they knew who Kate Smith was which proved that they could stay up quite late since Kate always sang both of their two TV stations off the air, around 12 Midnight, with "God

Bless America." Then to add to their maturity list, they had seen *Streetcar Named Desire* at the Ritz Theater—well, that is, until the action got too raw and graphic. Aunt Sue huffed and puffed, grabbed her big black signature purse, and made them leave early. Huddled together in the back seat, the girls whispered and imagined what they had missed, surmising the rest of the story all the way home.

Lila had quite a battle with her mother when she asked if she could go with Aunt Sue to her first seeing with Madame Holly. Her mother said, "Absolutely not, young missy. Such a waste of money to fill your head with pure nonsense. I can 'see' further than Madame Holly on any day of the week, including Sundays."

But what she did not see was that Lila, patient and stubbornly determined, could wheedle anyone into submission with the logic that cousin Bonnie was also going and Aunt Sue would pay for the family-rate entry fee. It seemed that Aunt Sue wanted a resolution from long-deceased Uncle Roland, saintly pastor of the Evangelical United Brethren Church.

With the velvet drapes pulled tight, the ancestor parlor was glowing luminescent; the glow was provided by the crystal globe at the center of the draped table. Aunt Sue, Bonnie, and Lila were sitting close together on one side of the little round table, waiting expectantly for what, they were not sure. Aunt Sue was nervous, you could tell by the twisting and beating she was rendering on her handkerchief; it was beginning to look like gift wrapping tissue paper that had cycled through three or four Christmas seasons. Lila noticed a sliver of the moon escaping into the room through a crack in a carelessly pulled drape on the east window. She wondered if she should get up and close it; she was pretty sure it was a lack of attention to detail. On the other hand, maybe that was Uncle Roland's entry portal and this was not her business. Aunt Sue also seemed extra on edge since she could not stretch her long legs under the table more than a couple of inches. When she peeked under, there appeared to be a black box, unmovable and firmly attached to the floor.

Soft ethereal music wafted down from the heavens above which made Lila wonder since she knew Violet's bedroom was approximately above this forbidden parlor. The music had a quiet relaxing effect on the three occupants, especially after some essence of lavender and patchouli came wafting into the room on the wings of what—angels perhaps. After all, Uncle Roland was not Catholic but he was called saintly. All three occasionally whispered to one another, and the two girls giggled nervously to each other. For comfort, they slid their chairs closer together so their knees could touch. Bonnie was next to her mom, and Lila sat next to Bonnie. Bonnie gave her mother a small tap on her hand and nodded at the disheveled hankie. Aunt Sue dropped her jowl and scowled at Bonnie but quickly relented. She dropped the hankie into her big black pocketbook and snapped her mouth and purse firmly shut.

The music was in a soft crescendo, gradually moving up to a fortissimo until it sounded like a queenly introduction when Madame Holly, adorned in multiple strands of purple beads and a black gauzy veil, waltzed lightly into the glowing room. The music and Madame settled back down to a simple pianissimo, and Madame was humming and chanting, organizing all her thoughts into some other-worldly state. Shivering, Bonnie slid half over onto her mother's chair, and cautiously, Lila slid half over onto Bonnie's chair, and the two girls found each other's hands. Finally Madame got down to business and began calling Uncle Roland down from somewhere, and Lila was still wondering if he might slip in through that crack in the curtain on a silver shaft from the moon which she could still see if she turned her head ever so slightly.

It was easy to see that Madame had contacted some higher spirits and they enjoyed communicating with her by lighting up the globe in answer to her probing questions. Madame was approaching near ecstasy by the time she turned to the business at hand. She reminded the spirits she would be calling the saintly Pastor Roland and how he was related to the participants at the table. With fluttering of the hands and a new chant, she whispered his name several times, only to be greeted by silence. Swiftly she switched to hymnal music and the spirits seemed to like this idea, and the essence wafting into the room had the faint odor of Old Spice shaving cream. The excitement was palpable, and the room seemed to be totally suffused with expectation and trepidation.

Uncle Roland did swing through for a twanging flyby and this ruffled the air and prickled the hair on the back of their necks, but it seemed he overshot since Madame had to call him back again. Lila peeked at the crack in the curtain which she swore had moved, just a little. Finally Uncle Roland swooped back in and consented to answer a few questions with a twang or by exciting Madame's globe. If you stared hard enough, you could swear that his face did appear in the globe when he spoke. At first, she asked simple questions that required a yes-or-no answer and he replied with a twang that did sound a little like a yes or no, especially with a little nudging from Madame. When Madame asked him how many souls he baptized by submersion in the Susquehanna River, the low rumble sounded like,: I don't remember. Anyway that was the way Madame interpreted it.

Finally Aunt Sue insisted that Madame ask him if he remembers cheating her on the exit fee that he charged each wagon leaving by her private road after his baptismal picnics on her private river landing. It appeared that Uncle Roland could not understand the question or did not want to answer as he disappeared into the night or left by the crack in the curtain. Even after several tries, Madame could not summon him back. She explained that this happens frequently when they do not wish to answer, but she was sure that on another night, he could be persuaded to be more cooperative. With that, Aunt Sue paid Madame her fee, grabbed up her purse and the girls, and scurried away, disgruntled and unsatisfied.

On the way home, Lila could tell that Aunt Sue was beyond disgruntled as her foot was way too heavy on the gas pedal. Lila asked if they would come in to help her tell mother about the experience as she knew that she would be peppered with all kinds of questions. They could help her out here. But no, they needed to get on home; so Bonnie and Lila exchanged their five-fingered handshake and Lila walked bravely into the house to face the inquisition. Funny thing was, her mother had only two questions. Lila explained that she did not see how much Aunt Sue gave Madame Holly, but she was now sure that Uncle Roland was good and gone and he would never be back to answer any more questions. Oh yes, and that Aunt Sue had just better give up and admit that she had been swindled.

Coming back from her reverie on the patio, chuckling, Lila made a mental note to quiz Violet how her mother managed to stage these seeings. Even if Violet had been sworn to secrecy back then, it would not matter now; Holly is gone. But enough for now, she must get up to the bee barn, her apiary, and get some much-needed work done before Violet's long visit. Her cherished childhood friend would be arriving in two days to spend a week. It had been years since her last visit, so they would have much ground to cover. Violet would do most of the talking with Lila mostly nodding. They were both now orphaned and widowed. She may not arrive on scheduled time due to driving a car with so many repairs that it is now unrecognizable. Several auto repair garages have refused her further service on "that Thar thing." Violet wants her car to make it into Ripley's Believe It or Not and is sure that Johnny Cash writes songs about her car. And maybe he does.

Lila was thinking back to grade school when she and Violet first discovered that they had an amazing ability to send each other silent messages. They were just starting multiplication and division problems in math. On the board, Mrs. Williams would give the children a long division problem to work out on their desks, then she would call on a student for the answer. Math was never Violet's strong point, so when she called on Violet for the answer, she was met with a stony moment of silence. As it happened, Lila really liked Violet, with her beautiful friendly smile, so she was hoping against hope that Violet would call out the answer. Lila put her head down and concentrated with all her might on the number 42. Within seconds, Violet called out forty-two. Suspiciously Mrs. Williams went around to the desk of the smart kid, directly in front of Violet, but he had come up with forty instead of forty-two. This surely did befuddle Mrs. Williams. Sitting one row over and two rows ahead, Lila turned around and Violet was smiling directly at her with a *"Thank you,"* and Lila stared back in amazement.

Finally with Benny at her heels, Lila made it up to the honeybee barn to inspect the activity around the six brood boxes and she noticed that the bee activity around Queen Mary's hive was not as robust as some of the others. She knew that very soon, she would have to break the propolis seal between the upper honey frames and the brood box to do an internal inspection. Perhaps she could make that inspection on Wednesday before Violet's visit. A small creak in the barn ceiling alerted Benny, and he cocked his ears to and fro. "Don't worry, Benny. The mice have to feed their little ones too."

Glancing up to see if any dust and chaff might be falling from the rafters, her eyes drifted down across the shelves holding the crates of this year's new crop of honey, carefully spun, bottled, and labeled. A shaft of sunlight struck the shelf which held the noncrated bottles, those intended for gifts and occasional barter with a neighbor. *Strange*, she thought, *I do not remember giving away that jar of honey that seems to be missing right there in the middle, and the entire lot seems to be a little more scattered than I would normally organize it. I need to put up an inventory sheet to track the honey supply line.*

"Come along, Benny, we have work to do down at the house. It would be nice if we could just live outdoors and slip into the bee barn when the weather chills. That would suit you, wouldn't it? Thank you for always agreeing with me. Most people don't."

Lila sighed at her list of chores that needed attention before Violet arrived. Drano in kitchen sink, wood for fireside chats, scrub grunge from shower, wash guest towels, freshen the guest bedroom, and rake the mud out of the mudroom. Lila is not pretentious, but when she compares her lot with old friends, she does have her standards; she does not want to come up short—well, not by much anyway. On the way down the flowered path to the house, Lila snipped off a few cosmoses for the robin egg blue vase. Blue is Violet's favorite color. The cosmos path was a favorite of Lila's mother, and she rejuvenated it first when she returned to claim her inheritance. Lila took a leave of absence from the Brookfield Chemical Plant and was enjoying her new lifestyle. She occasionally returned to the plant as a consultant just to keep her options open, and it added a little income.

After the scrubbing was done, Lila penciled out a tentative schedule for the next few days and made a grocery list. She was anxious to have this visit go well; it meant a lot to her. She knew that she would have to honor previously scheduled commitments while Violet was here, so it would take some planning for things to go smoothly. For one, she had previously agreed to meet with her neighbor, Jewel, to plan their trip to Erie. Jewel wanted Lila to take her to Erie to see the Barnum and Bailey Circus Spectacular so she could connect with some of her old friends. Years ago and fifty pounds lighter, fifteen-year-old Jewel ran away with the circus and had a brief jewel-studded career before her mom and daddy located her and dragged her back home. As the story goes, in a skimpy costume, she rode the last elephant in the opening ceremony. And many times, Lila had heard the whispered rumor that Jewel was being trained for the bareback equestrian event. It was also said that Jewel had some gypsy background a generation or two in the past. Since the circus event was several weeks away, this meeting could be postponed until after Violet's visit.

The most worrisome of her commitments, however, were her continuing sessions with Marguerite. Jed, owner of the local breakfast and lunch café, had asked her to befriend Marguerite and help her with some broken equipment in her alternative medicine laboratory. Marguerite had apparently managed to help Jed's grandson after doctors had failed. In order to earn a little money so she could replace broken lab equipment, Marguerite took a job in the café prep room on Tuesday and Thursday mornings. Being naturally curious about alternative medicine, Lila touched base with her there, helped her peel potatoes, and felt that they were becoming friends. Lila thought this project was intriguing since she knew of rumors about someone practicing witchcraft over in the Hollow. This might be one and the same person. Jed had told her that Marguerite lived over in a secluded enclave in the East Valley. Lila wondered how she might have secured a job at Jed's Café and who her contacts might have been, but Jed seemed to be very protective of this information. Well, Lila was a patient sort and she knew that sooner or later, she would hear more.

Day 2: Tuesday

Early the next morning, with rooster George crowing with gusto, Lila jumped out of bed, taking inventory of her sore muscles from cleaning and shining. She was not afraid of manual labor, but she was not particularly fond of routine housework. The banished dirt and grime just seeped back in through the cracks and settled into the same crevices, finding its own comfort zone. Give her a barn repair any day or gardening chores, those projects had some lasting satisfaction. But due to yesterday's whirlwind cleaning, the house was good enough for company and she was ready should Violet arrive sometime tomorrow o'clock. Lila chuckled, thinking that it was surprising that Violet did not make her meet halfway as was their habit in their childhood bicycle days.

Lila splashed water on her face, combed her hair with her damp fingers, looked in the mirror, and said, "Good enough for Jed's Café."

She would pass on the at-home coffee as Jed always brought her a cup to the back between the crates of potatoes. Marguerite would be there peeling, chopping, and anticipating her arrival. Lila wished that Jed would allow her to come through the backdoor as Marguerite was accustomed to, but Jed said since Lila was not paid help, she had to enter through the front like proper people. So Lila felt obligated to dress in town clothing instead of her familiar farm attire. Today she chose clean olive-green slacks and a light-yellow blouse. Noticing soil on the sleeve, she covered it over with a warm salmon-colored sweater. She knew that Rachel and her discerning tsk-tsk gang would be there for the pass-through inspection. Besides it was not toasty warm back in the prep pantry; sometimes she had to keep her jacket on while peeling and chopping with Marguerite.

Lila boxed up two dozen carefully washed eggs for Jed and a jar of honey for Marguerite, found her keys, gave Benny a pat, and dashed out the door. This morning, Doozie, her second-hand red Jeep, started up with only a small complaint; it was in good repair, thanks to a skilled mechanic down on Latimer Street. When she brought it in for inspection for the first time, Dave said, "Well, what a Doozie!" And the name stuck.

He offered to purchase Doozie for a fair price, but Lila knew he was only teasing. The Jeep had a very useful tow bar package which she needed for towing supplies from the Bevin Bee Supply store in Sylvania. Dave would barter the labor costs for honey but not the cost of parts. Still quite a bargain, what with the exorbitant cost of labor these days.

Carefully avoiding the empty space in front of the café beside Rachel's Pontiac Bonneville, Lila found a spot hidden around to the side, between two familiar pickup trucks, a Ford and a Chevy. Lila smiled knowing that Burt and Sonny would be occupied, arguing the merits of their *ride*. It was always Burt who called attention to Lila's entrance as she tried to slide in unnoticed. "Hey, bee lady, how are we buzzing today, huh?"

Lila acknowledged Burt with a slight nod and continued to the prep room door. With coffee cups in various states of suspension, Rachel and Gang rolled their eyes, in turn, like a line of cascading dominoes in Lila's direction. Only Sylvie looked down in embarrassment. Ringleader and gossip queen, Rachel, was sure that there was somethin' going on between Jed and Lila and she would count how many times Jed swooped into the prep kitchen after Lila arrived.

Lila tried to take the most direct route to the prep pantry but the tables were always pushed around such that each day, a new route was required. Jed, in a gently soiled apron, glanced up from the sizzling bacon grill and poured two cups of coffee, one for Lila with extra cream and one for Marguerite with a tiny bit of cream. He came over and acknowledged Lila with a slight nod, retrieved the two dozen eggs, gave her the two coffees, and held the pantry door open with warm deference. Marguerite was there, peeling potatoes, and almost audibly humming a chant, one that probably had reverence and spirituality. Peering down into her coffee cup, Marguerite winced at the sight of the cream-lightened coffee. "Now, Mar, you know Jed is only trying to get some calcium to your bones," Lila said in a soothing voice. "And look! I brought you some more honey for your elixirs."

Mar did not refuse the honey and carefully placed the cloth-wrapped package in her canvass traveling sack. Lila smiled when she noticed a familiar pink collar peeking out from under Mar's heavy gray sweatshirt.

Session over and gauntlet run, Lila picked up Benny and headed over to Alma, the nearest town with a full-service grocery store.

Rockton's miniature local grocery store would not have the items that Violet would tolerate; although that may have changed since their last visit. Oh well, no matter, Lila wanted to stop at Shanebrooks Boutique for a new yellow blouse. If she took the hardpack back road through Goshen, she could make a quick stop to check on Mrs. Swanson and drop off some honey. It never ceased to amaze her how grand the Swanson house looked, gracefully aging with tinges of gray; it still reigned as queen of the hill. Perched precisely overlooking the tiny hamlet of Goshen and the old vacated Stanton homestead, it had the best view of the neighborhood. The dowager within, Mrs. Swanson, would meet her at the side porch with the door partly closed behind her with only a toehold to keep it from locking. Lila often wondered what she was hiding behind that door. Benny always liked to stop and get his homemade doggie treat. Many times, Lila suggested to Mrs. Swanson that she should consider marketing her doggie treats, but she would just smile and say, "Oh, *go on!*" It always seemed to Lila that so many folks around here could use a little extra cash, but of course, it was well-known that Mrs. Swanson had inherited a tidy sum.

It was a slow day at Shanebrooks, so the clerks were overanxious to help which made Lila a little nervous as she was paying for a green blouse instead of yellow. Oh well, not to worry, her skin tone preferred green. She allowed leashed Benny to lead her to the pet store where she purchased dog food and a new toy. Benny said please to the nice young man at the register, and by canine magic, this produced a new treat. Benny gave him a thank you and tucked the rawhide bone between his jowls. Back in the car, the rawhide gave him some entertainment while Lila went to the grocery store. Food supplies tucked away in Doozie, she allowed herself a very quick stop at the coffee house for a Caffé Misto. Jed would scoff at the high price for a suspicious mix of coffee and milk, ceremoniously run through a fancy machine, just to charge a fancy price. She does not tell Jed about this adulterous affair.

Back home, she and Benny made a quick dash to call the chickens into the henhouse for the night to protect them from coyotes. Benny dashed around, herding hens as if they were sheep; but George, the major domo here, gave him riotous chase, proud and reluctant to head on up to his tree roost. With the eggs gathered from the laying boxes and the door latched, they made a quick check into the bee barn where all was quiet, except for several inquisitive guard bees checking identity cards. Lila took a moment to rearrange the shelf of noncrated gift jars of honey. On a nail next to this shelf, she hung up a list with a pencil tied to a string to keep track of the gifted jars. She counted the loose jars, marked the date, and penciled in—Marguerite-1 and Mrs. Swanson-1. Lila was happy about the $103.33 which she received from the Alma Grocery Store for a crate of twenty-four one-pound jars of honey. This account was carefully marked down in a spiral notebook rather than on a file program on her new Apple IIe computer. She knew, however, that one day, she would be using all this new technology that Silicon Valley was madly producing just for her. On a rainy day, or next winter, she would take the time to figure it all out and make the switch—well, maybe.

After putting together a quick meal for Benny and some leftovers for herself, she settled down in front of a tiny two-log fire and read *The Art of Alchemy*, hoping to aid her conversations with Marguerite. For one thing, she wanted to know why honey elixirs required so much honey for such a few ounces of tonic. Lila hoped that Marguerite was as least fermenting the remainder and sediments into a tasty mead. A fermented drink should bring in more income than medicinal elixirs which Mar tended to give away. Surely her grandfather had taught her the art of fermentation many years ago.

The Art of Alchemy was a tough book to read for Lila; it used many of the same scientific chemical names as she learned in high school chemistry, but they meant, altogether, different parts of the medicinal plants. Alchemy is a laborious and time-consuming practice. But she did reap an aha moment. The honeybee puts the alchemist several weeks ahead by collecting the nectar and pollen from the blossom, alleviating the need to collect the plant, and then the bees proceed to concentrate and preserve the product until the alchemist can distill and fractionate it into the medical solutions and tonics. Lila thought about the face hydrating cream she was concocting with honey and avocado and thought she might ask Marguerite if she had any suggestion.

Day 3: Wednesday

"Good morning, Benny," Lila mumbled. "Up early, are we? George must be sleeping in this morning or we slept right through his morning ruckus."

Benny did three quick revolutions to tell Lila that she was three times behind in the morning chores and that she had better get a move on. Benny was extremely smart, intuitive, and good at telling time. He could count up to three days for sure as Lila had experience with this. He also intuited that something new was going to happen soon as Lila had been acting a little off-kilter these past few days, what with getting ready for Violet's visit and fussing over his muddy paws.

As Lila prepared breakfast and coffee, a "For Sale" sign kept flashing across her mind's eye. Bringing this memory to the fore, she realized that she saw it yesterday, over in Goshen, while passing the old homestead where Violet grew up. The sign was partially hidden by clinging overgrown vines which were also reclaiming the small outbuildings. The back porch had fallen in, but the rest of the house looked firm of foundation. This house had once been home to many happy memories, including toe-tapping musical hoedowns. It was practically screaming for someone to rescue it.

The main barn was leaning toward Swanson's but still standing. In fact, when Lila thought about it, she remembered that the barn always leaned toward Swanson's. Lila did not think much about this familiar old landmark on the drive-by yesterday; but now, she wondered if Mrs. Swanson would know who currently owned the place. It would occupy a whole day if she and Violet could tour the house and grounds and reminisce over a picnic lunch on the old flagstone veranda, a pretty impressive patio in its day. Also maybe, just maybe, this might set Violet thinking about a move back home. Well, maybe.

"Okay, Benny, enough dawdling for now." Lila reassured him that they would start their chores by pulling on her soiled canvas barn coat. Benny kept close track of that coat since he would always be included in its walkabout and chores around the bee farm and Lilaland. After regular chores were attended to, they would do some prep work for the little bridge which she was building in order to have a dry crossing over Alder Run. She would hitch Doozie up to the trailer and load in some old timbers which she found down behind the old foundry here in Rockton. No one seemed to mind when she relieved them of the mess. In fact, one old gent thanked her for cleaning up the place. She reasoned that Violet would be game to hold some boards while she nailed and hammered since that was what they did back in their day. Vinnie, a neighbor, had already helped her place the foundation blocks and stones on both sides of the run to stabilize the future bridge. The distance across at this location was the narrowest site that she could find. In dry summers, when the run was down to a trickle, crossing was a few easy hops on strategically placed stones; but in early spring, when the maple sap was running, it could be several feet deep.

She had some handsome maple sugar trees up on the next slope, and she had promised Vinnie that he could run his tap line there next year. Lila already bartered honey for maple syrup, ounce for ounce, but Vinnie persistently argued that she was getting the better deal since her bees concentrated their nectar while he had to boil the sap into syrup. Now she reasoned, if Vinnie collected sap from her trees, then she should receive a sweeter bargain. Anyway that would give them a good arguing point since Vincent loved to argue. And she could probably secretly share a little with Marguerite for her elixirs. If Marguerite needed the raw sap instead of the syrup, then she would look for another solution. Alternatively she had a big maple sugar tree down by the barn that Vinnie could tap for her. This sap she could give to Marguerite straightaway as she did not wish to get into the art of syrup making. Beekeeping, chicken husbandry, and a vegetable garden provided enough demands on her time.

Around noon, the sun was shining and the air was calm, always a good time to work with the bees as the majority of the worker bees would be out foraging for nectar and pollen from the peach and apple blossoms today. Lila could smell the sweet blossoms, and her sneezing was kicking into gear. Sneezing was always difficult when cocooned into a bee hat, so she learned to wear a carpenter's dust mask under the bee hat. Many days, when simply checking on the hives and state of honey production, she did not have to suit up as the honeybee is quite tolerant. Today she would be opening brood box number 6—Queen Mary's domain; the nurse bees always take offense with this activity, then they get the guard bees excited. Mary must be aging out and not laying vigorously. The nurse bees know how to prepare for a new queen in the event of queen loss, and they also know how to speed up the aging queen's demise. Of course, they can do this without any outside help, but Lila and Queen Mary had restarted this bee farm together; and now, Lila wanted to say her goodbyes, if necessary. Fortunately the queens in hives 1 through 5 were quite vigorous and fertile.

In the bee barn, Lila suited up in white and gathered several tools needed for breaking the propolis seal between the brood box and the upper honey boxes. On inspection, the upper honey frames were partially filled but not as amply as in the other hives. Down in the brood box, all ten frames were filled with moderate activity with the nursery in various stages of pupa gestation, plus evidence of many new queen cells being constructed which may indicate a failing queen. Relentlessly the guard bees continued to give warning by batting at her white-veiled bee hat. Finally with apprehensive joy, she did locate Queen Mary who seemed quite alive and fit on inspection and able to give Lila an eye to eye chat. "So we carry on together a little longer, huh?" Lila inquired.

Queen Mary turned, waggled her fanny, and went back to her queenly duties. Satisfied with the encounter, Lila closed up the brood box and knew the guard bees would reseal it properly within a day or two. After the hive settled down, Lila called Benny to let him know all was safe now. Benny was stung on the nose one time, so he was not keen to hang around opened hives. He had learned that the white hat means just that.

Satisfied that she could be patient now and look forward to Violet's visit, she and Benny sat quietly for a time in the bee barn, making plans. She would call Jewel and postpone their meeting until after Violet returned home. Perhaps she could skip the sessions with Marguerite while Violet was here, but then again, it may fit in okay. Violet could have breakfast at Jed's and could have a look around to determine if she spotted anyone she might remember or if she saw any distant relatives from Goshen. Most of Violet's relatives had moved away, so this was not likely. However, she had a very outgoing personality so others might recognize her as someone from their past. As a very young girl, Violet pumped out copious accordion tunes while playing in her father's bluegrass and square dance band. As soon as she was big enough to handle the accordion, around nine years of age, she was put to the keyboard. At nine years, however, the accordion still looked bigger than she.

Violet's musical talent came directly down from Wales, through many generations. Lila wondered if Violet ever had the chance to dance. She would remember to ask her. As a young girl, Violet was a bundle of talent but not much for the books, just a polar opposite to Lila; but together, they made a complete guidance system. Lila was grounded by earth's magnetic spin and Violet flew by the stars. She had more street smarts than all the young girls in Goshen, Rockton, and Alma combined, mostly due to her father's lifestyle which often took them on various road trips for music festivals and homecomings. Another favorite of her dad's was religious revival meetings which made Lila's father smirk. "Ah yes! Revival meetings where more souls are made than saved."

And one could never be sure to which religion they claimed as their own. It was said that they were searching for one that suited their freewheeling lifestyle. Being away from home for large chunks of time did interfere with Violet's advancement in school. She was two years older than Lila; however, by the fourth grade, Lila had caught up to her, at least in book knowledge. Or should it be said, Violet waited for Lila to catch up.

"Well, Benny, we better get on down to the house in case Violet does have some problem on the road with that Thar Thing and tries to call us," Lila said, urging Benny out of his reverie.

She took a little time tidying the honey shelves; then they headed back down the path to the charming stone-faced two-story cottage. The house was cozy and warm on this fresh spring evening, smelling of blossoms and honey-crafted soaps. Also she had placed homemade sachets of lavender and Russian sage into each closet to camouflage any damp smell wafting from the basement. There was still much to be done with her old cottage, but it was in usable and reliable repair with all-new plumbing and heating systems. She changed the needy smoke-belching coal furnace over to a modern oil-fired furnace. Firing, tending, and banking that coal-eating monster was way too demanding for Lila's current lifestyle. When Lila could secure a little extra cash, she planned to remodel the first-floor bathroom and install one on the second floor as well. The roof had been inspected and pronounced sound for now anyway.

Thinking about all that was needed here at her cottage gave her pause about Violet's ability to even consider buying back her homestead over in Goshen. Still maybe, at one time, Violet had a teen crush on Vinnie; and here he is, single again. He may see the prospect of new project, the house fix-up and Violet in the bargain, that is. Hopefully Violet has the same sweet smile and wonderful striking pose. But Vinnie has stopped inquiring about Violet. Vinnie and Violet—now there is a match for the poets. Or should it be, t'other way 'round—Violet and Vinnie. Vinnie was several years older than Lila, but she remembered that he had a number of girlfriends back in the day. Dashing football star and all-around athlete. His dad had a construction business, and he worked for his dad on weekends so he had some extra spending cash—and a car!

After a bowl of homemade soup, Lila settled in with *The Art of Alchemy* and Benny sniffed out his rawhide bone hidden under her chair. She was only on chapter 2 and finding it increasingly mystifying but fascinating. The preparation of medicinal tonics is an ancient art, first practiced in India, China, and Egypt. From Egypt, the practice spread rapidly up through Eastern Europe then France. All alchemists, of every religious persuasion, believed that there was a need for reverence during the laborious preparations to bring purified essences out of their distillations and condensations. Many of the preparations required at least a biblical month for the proper methodology. That info alone might open up dialog with reticent Marguerite, a homeschooled alchemist. Also Lila wanted to ask her if we had the plant, horsetail, growing in this region. She thought that she remembered her grandmother grinding it and putting it into a salve to treat skin rashes. And this book claims that horsetail corrects and maintains the organic calcium equilibrium.

Lila remembered from her biochemistry classes that ancient Egyptian and Greek traditional medicine utilized extracts of willow bark and myrtle leaves to treat aches, pains, and fevers. And yes, we now know they both contain salicylic acid which has been formulated into one of the most cost-effective drugs ever produced—*aspirin*. And there are now other examples of modern drugs being formulated from traditional mendicants because someone took the time to translate and research some very ancient Chinese manuscripts. A chemical, artemisinin, found in the herb wormwood was described in an ancient fourth-century Chinese formula which is now known to be effective against malaria.

Putting her book aside, Lila started to think ahead about Violet's visit. Lila pondered, *How will I explain to Violet why she cannot go back to the pantry with me? Marguerite is not ready to be questioned by an outsider. I am just beginning to gain Marguerite's confidence and I do not want that progress interrupted. Violet, on the other hand, would take it in stride since she had been exposed to many worldly practices in her day, and after all, what was in that pouch which Violet wore around her neck so many years ago? Did I sometimes get a tiny whiff of garlic? And I remember the time she wore that rabbit's foot for days on end—something about bringing good luck.*

"Humph!" Lila's mother said. "The only luck it brought was bad luck for the rabbit." Then Lila remembered the time that her Mexican jumping bean disappeared the same day that Violet had been over for a visit. Her well-traveled cousin brought her that jumping bean all the way from Mexico, and she was dismayed by the loss but would not allow her mother to blame Violet. Violet's friendship meant more than that there ole bean.

It was 10:00 p.m. and no Violet and no call. Of course, she does not believe in telephones, but her son called twice. He reassured Lila not to worry since Mom could always take care of herself. Lila believed that more fervently than the son. However, that Thar Thing might have let her down in some desolate place. Knowing that Violet could easily drive the nine hours nonstop, she was pretty sure that she would make it in yet tonight, but Lila was receiving a thought wave *"car trouble"*. Her mother always said that the two of them did not need telephones since Violet could send her signals over the airwaves by telepathy. She left the porch light on, the door unlocked, and a note telling Violet to wake her. She climbed into bed, turned out the light, and fell asleep.

At 1:00 a.m., she answered the ringing phone with a hasty, "Where are you?"

To this abrupt salutation, Vinnie retorted, "That was what I was going to ask you."

He was on his way home from his nightcap at Buster's and saw the porch light on. "Vinnie, I am waiting for Violet to arrive, and I left a light on. I should have told you she was coming to spend the week. I hope you can join us for dinner one night while she is here," Lila said hopefully.

"Well, maybe," Vinnie responded hesitantly. "We will see. I am pretty busy right now, installing a kitchen over in Alma, and of course, you understand I am building some benches for the grand opening of the new library."

"Vinnie," Lila said sternly, "I am sure you can spare one free evening to see an old friend." She knew this sounded like a demand, but after all, she had helped him with visitors from time to time, even offering a spare bedroom. Lila went back to bed and slept restlessly, thinking that it was going to be a short five hours when George announces sunrise.

At 2:30 a.m., Lila was startled awake with lights from the driveway flashing onto her bedroom wall. Bouncing up and racing to the window, she saw Violet jumping down from the passenger side of a pickup with some lettering on the door. Lila could not make out the words, but the pickup was white with orange lettering like the trucks used by the guards over at the federal prison, some thirty-six miles away. Her father had worked there as an instructor, and sometimes, he caught rides with the regulars. She heard Violet thanking the driver as he lugged her big suitcase from the back of the truck. And she thought she heard the driver say that he would pick her up on the way to work tomorrow so she could deal with her car. Lila raced downstairs, missed a step, and slid down the last two on her spine. There was a tricky curve in the staircase, near the bottom, where three of the turning steps were small and triangular shape and, as Vinnie would say, "not up to code." She shook off the mishap and ran for the door just as Violet was letting herself into the entry and dragging in her suitcase.

Both a little rattled, they stopped to stare, to assess each other and tally up what they had missed in each other's absence. Finally Violet broke into her winning smile and threw open her arms for the ritual hug. Stepping back one pace but still holding hands, both women rushed to talk at the same time, stumbling over all the missed years of real conversation, the face-to-face kind. Violet apologized for coming in so late. She had a late start because her son came by to tell her that if she waited a week, he would come with her. "I guess he thinks I am over the hill, almost fifty."

Lila did notice that Violet was still quite lovely but just a little tired from the drive and thinner than she expected.

Lila really wanted to know if she had been frightened hiking up to the prison gate in the wee hours of the morning to find someone to help. Violet said, well, yes, a little, but it was well-lit and she could see several guards on duty at the gatehouse. And she remembered that this small local prison only incarcerated white-collar criminals, far from really dangerous; it was known for taking in misbehaving lawyers, bankers, and politicians. But Lila said that she heard another story; due to overcrowding at the western prison, they had agreed to move some more dangerous convicts to the local prison. But that could possibly be only talk because she did not see anything in the paper; but then, they like to keep these types of things quiet, don't they?

Finally they came to their senses and decided to call it a night, knowing that in the morning, they could figure out who would talk first. They did agree that as a priority in the morning, they would go down to talk to Dave, Lila's mechanic, to see how soon he could go over to fix or tow Violet's car. Lila also thought that it might be wise to warn him about the car's history.

The Visit

Day 1: Thursday

With Violet sleeping soundly, Lila put on a pot of coffee and filled the tea kettle with fresh spring water which she dipped from the nearby springhouse. In this valley region, many of the old homesteads were built purposely near one of these springs which the farmers cleverly captured in a four-by-four mortared foundation and attached an overflow drain leading into a cement trough. Then they protected it from marauding creatures by building a small springhouse over the entire arrangement. The cool running water in the trough provided refrigeration for milk, butter, and cheese. Lila was lucky that her great-grandfather was clever enough to have cemented the floor in his springhouse. Back in the day, before refrigeration, her great-grandmother must have been impressed with her clever husband.

Benny and Lila hurriedly let the chickens out of the henhouse, gave a wave to suspicious George, and then made a quick pass by the vegetable garden. The early vegetables, kohlrabi, onions, and peas, were growing nicely, but the tender vegetables needed to be planted soon. Her growing season was short. Oh well, if there was time, perhaps Violet might help her later in the week. If not, no one would notice a few less zucchinis on the planet. But wait, Lila had a feeling that something was wrong. Recapturing the moment when the hens scrambled out, she remembered that bossy Henrietta was not the first hen out the door this morning, so they hurried back to the henhouse and could not find her.

"Benny, wasn't Henrietta there last night when we closed the door?" she queried.

Benny looked confused and sniffed around. Lila felt a little uneasy but decided she would have to worry about this problem later. They hurried back to the house to wake up Violet. Dave was an early riser and a very busy mechanic; they needed to touch base with him before his book filled up. For want of timing, Lila also decided that she would take Violet with her to Jed's where Violet could get a decent breakfast while she was tending to the session with Marguerite. She had some special info to share with Mar and she did not want to miss this opportunity. Carefully she gave Violet cautious warning not to interrupt the session, fearing that her added presence would give Marguerite pause about their privacy.

Reluctantly Lila tiptoed into the guest room and gently opened the blinds as she was thinking that this was not how she expected their first day to unfold. Violet stirred and said, "I hope you are not expecting me to drink that foul coffee concoction which I smell wafting across my nose."

"No, Violet dear, fresh spring water tea is brewing for you, your favorite sassafras from our very own roots."

Violet responded, "Oh, thank goodness, you remembered."

Lila proudly retorted, "Yes, we harvested just last week in your honor."

Violet thought how nice it was to be pampered as she jumped out of bed and quickly dressed without showering. She was a little anxious to check out Dave's schedule and arrange to bring her car back to Rockton.

As Violet was giving Dave a description of her car, which she abandoned on the road last night, Dave rolled conspiratorial eyes at Lila. Lila tried to keep a smile from edging into the conversation. She wanted to seriously impress on Dave that she needed this favor, and she brought a gift package of homemade goods and honey. The work staff was already devouring the honey and nut kuchen back in the lunchroom. Lila's honey kuchen was an honored gift. Finally Dave agreed to tow the car back to Rockton by tomorrow night. Then he would "have a look." Oh yes, he would, thought Lila, quite a look!

As they pulled into the café parking lot, she was somewhat relieved to see two familiar pickups which meant Burt and Sonny would be there holding court. Of course, she noticed Rachel's Bonneville as well. She reminded Violet that she was not even to peek into the prep pantry and she held out a good-behavior carrot of a special meal at Michael's. On the one hand, Michael's was locally famous; on the other hand, it was the only restaurant in Rockton open after 2:00 p.m. Drafting up her courage and putting on her confident face, she turned to Violet and gave her a wink and a nod. In response, Violet spread her left hand submissively. Some things never change; the two old friends could still communicate volumes without a word being passed.

All chatter stopped when the two women entered, even Burt was speechless for once. Lila was suddenly conscious of the fact that Violet, with her still-natural blond hair and winning smile, did offer newsworthy gossip for Rockton. Lila sensed a moment of pride, knowing that she held the reins to this show; after all, she was the organizer of this event. Violet, being accustomed to the effect she made in these situations, took it all in stride. Lila gently nudged her to a table in the corner as far away from Rachel's gang as she could, but this seated her only two tables away from Burt and Sonny's appraising eyes. Sonny slipped his cap down onto his lap, and he brushed his thinning hair back over his forehead. *Well, you ole fool,* thought Lila, *you never took your hat off for me.* At least Burt, with cap still on, acknowledged her with a slight nod, but with eyes sparking, he went back to studying this new phenomenon. The number of photons and free electrons bouncing between the Formica tables that morning spoke silent volumes, and Lila lowered her eyelids to protect her retina. It was enough to make her a disciple of Marconi. Waitress Bonnie, in her ponytail, was unusually quick with pad and pencil and motioned for Lila to look over at Jed who had no coffee cups at the ready and a worried look. Lila quickly learned that Marguerite did not show up for work and did not send a message. Seeing Jed's concern, Lila tossed the morning newspaper on Violet's table, brushed past Jed to the prep room, and put on Mar's apron and started to peel while she waited for Marguerite to appear.

While scraping, peeling, and chopping, Lila tried to catch snatches of conversation seeping under the ill-fitted pantry door. She heard references to Crazy Stanton and his wild escapades. She was sure they were reminding Violet of the time that her father, Cliff Stanton—better known as Crazy Stanton—went out to Ohio and brought back a hot-air balloon, used of course. He tethered it to a very long rope, taught himself how to fly it. Then when he screwed up his courage, he took off on a day when the gentle northwest wind would sweep him over to Apple Valley, a landing site with manicured farm fields. However, there were several apple orchards between the launch and this prime landing spot. There are now several stories as to what went wrong and how many farmers and wagons were summoned to extricate the entire catastrophe from the pumpkin-sweet apple tree into which Stanton crashed. Bottom line, the balloon nylon and Stanton's pride were shredded that day. This ended his ballooning days but not his desire to learn to fly. Cliff Stanton was sure that there was a used Piper Cub somewhere with his name on it. He believed that he was meant to soar either through his music or by wings. As reckless and reverent as he was, some people assumed he would soon soar with real wings.

Just as Marguerite hustled in through the backdoor, Lila could hear Violet warming up with some Stanton stories of her own which she was eager to embellish as time passed. Even Rachel's coffee went cold as she strained with rapt attention. With Mar's session over and the peeling done, Lila went out to collect Violet who's tab had been paid for by some anonymous admirer. With a smile and wave, they hurried for home. Lila was worried about Henrietta.

The two quickly changed into barn clothes and waterproof mucking boots since Lila wanted to look for Henrietta and show Violet the bridge preparations at Alder Run. Violet was excited as a schoolgirl since it brought back so many memories of their young excursions, and Benny was excited to have so much attention. They started close to the henhouse, looking for signs of animal tracks to no avail since it had been drying for a couple of days. Searching and clucking near the henhouse, they located only eight hens and George—with no sign of Henrietta. Benny, sniffing around, begged to go faster and further, but Lila cautioned him to slow down. Finally they were in despair and decided to head on up to Alder Run. On the path to the run, Violet found a deep-bronze feather caught in a wild honeysuckle bush and Lila confirmed that it looked like one of Henrietta's. This still did not mean much, however, since chicken feathers could be found anywhere. They agreed to continue on the path with their eyes open for foul play. The quarter-mile path from the henhouse to the run was an easy walk through a stand of shady pines. And for a moment, Henrietta was forgotten as Lila told Violet about the bridge plans and Vinnie's help with the foundation. A little too eagerly, Violet suggested that they should invite Vinnie when they went to Michael's for dinner.

Since it was late spring, the run was still several feet deep and to cross, even here, jumping from slippery stone to slippery stone, looked like disaster. After brief eye contact, both women sat down on the bank and removed socks and boots before crossing to the other side. After inspecting and criticizing the foundation on the other side, Violet noted some changes that should be made before they started the bridge construction.

After pulling on their boots, Violet suggested that they should hike further up the path to look for evidence of chicken feathers and discarded bones. Lila did not like the sound of what she was implying but went along with the suggestion as the pull of the hill on her middle-age thighs was good exercise, even though Violet certainly did not need it. They went on up to inspect and estimate the number of maple sugar trees that Vinnie planned to tap next year. They stopped before they reached the plateau at the top where some exhausted coal strippings had been abandoned many years ago. Many neighborhood kids, including Violet and Lila, learned to swim in one of the water holes produced by coal removal. On the way back down to the run, Violet consoled Lila that maybe Henrietta was safely back at the henhouse, but even she did not sound convinced.

After a change of clothes, Lila asked Violet to join her for iced tea on the little patio off the kitchen. In honor of this visit, Lila had purchased some second-hand wrought iron furniture and covered the stained cushions with a handsome spring flowered pattern. Well, at least two cushions were done in time. Two to go. The nice thing about getting ready for company is that it makes one do some things that should have been done long ago.

Just as they were making plans for the next day, Dave called and asked to talk to Violet. From the gist of the conversation, Lila figured out that he had already towed Violet's car home and needed to discuss some problems, meaning costs, etc., before he even began to have a serious look into repairs. "And by the way, who had been doing the work on your car? He deserves a medal!" Lila and Violet decided that it would be best if they dropped by Dave's right away as time might be of the essence to get Violet back home next week for some medical tests.

Dave was out in the back under a new-looking Buick, just hauled in from the highway by AAA. When Lila asked Dave's new receptionist if she would call Dave to the desk, she was professionally brisk and told them they would have to wait. Would they care for a cup of coffee? Well, a new receptionist and now coffee. Lila was thinking that maybe they were paying Dave too much. But then, the next option would be to take their repair business over to Alma. So they sat down to wait, Lila with coffee and Violet with calming tea. When Lila thought about it, she was the one who needed the calming and wished that she liked tea. Dave arrived with a stern look on his face which noticeably softened when his eyes landed on Violet. She definitely had that effect—and not just on men; it was universal. They had some serious discussion about timing, ordering of parts, and an upfront down payment. Clearly Dave was worried about that last issue the most. Behind Violet's back, Lila signaled Dave with a dismissive shake of her head that he was not to worry about the money angle.

Back at the cottage, just at sunset bee time, Lila and Violet each carried a glass of wine up to the bee barn to watch the pollen-laden bees returning for the night. During apple blossom season, their golden-orange pollen sacs were so heavy that they hovered and zigzagged down to the crowded landing board in order to prevent a crash landing. Lila never grew tired of watching her girls coming home from a hard day's work.

Several years ago, after an extremely cold winter, Lila lost five of her seven hives, and she wanted to prevent further disasters due to freezing temperature. After some research, she decided to install her hives into the barn wall with the bee entry face oriented toward the outside, but the bulk of the hive was under cover inside the barn. That way, she did not have to worry about wintertime insulation in this sometimes-frigid climate or the occasional black bear pitching the hive over in search of honey. Also this arrangement allowed her to work with the bees undercover and open up the hive without letting cold drafts stir them into a frenzy.

Of course, Lila's local bee mentor told her that by placing the hives so close together, that she might encourage robber bees to steal honey from adjacent hives. And this could happen, but so far, she had not seen it as a problem. Somehow the guard bees know who belongs and who doesn't. Anyway there was a plentiful nectar source that kept the workers zipping out to the orchards all day long, except on rainy days when they mostly huddled inside their hive. He also said that the bees might become a little disoriented trying to find their own hive, "Like a drunk coming home to tract housing where all the houses look pretty much alike. Some men don't know they slept in the wrong house until morning." Lila figured that her bees were more discerning than some men.

On the outside of the bee barn, Lila had set up an observatory patio with redwood chairs so one could watch the bee traffic. Violet was fascinated with this arrangement as she remembered that Lila's mother lined up her hives on foundation stones, completely exposed to the elements. As the sun waned and a chill set in, they went down to call in the hens, all but missing Henrietta, and returned to the house to a warm vegetable soup for supper.

By the tiny two-log fire that night, the two friends covered a wide variety of subjects as both were anxious to be brought up to date. For one thing, Lila knew that Violet was a vegetarian because she could not bring herself to eat anything with a face. Thank goodness, Mother Nature did not think to put faces on roots, grasses, and vegetables, or at least, not what we think of as a face. Lila knew that some vegetarians moved on up to vegans. That would make cooking for her friend more difficult; after all, this was an egg farm and Lila liked to cook with eggs and butter. No, Violet reassured her that even though she toyed with the idea, she had not yet embraced the vegan concept.

Lila had several new hearty vegetarian recipes ready for menus this week, and the local restaurant had a nice vegetarian entree. That discussion reminded the two to make plans for the dinner at Michael's. Violet was anxious that they should invite Vinnie as Lila had promised. Lila decided that perhaps Violet should make the call since they were old friends, even dated several times in the past. Reluctantly Violet did make the call, and Vinnie said that he could meet them there on Saturday night. Violet sat back down, looking pleased with that result. The timing was excellent since Lila hoped to show Violet her childhood homestead over in Goshen and present the idea that she might purchase the old farm for a song. Of course, her mind was racing ahead as to how Vinnie might figure into the picture, but she was trying not to get too optimistic.

As the hour was getting late, they decided to call it a day and planned to go over to Goshen tomorrow and have a look around. Comfortably sinking down into bed that night, Lila decided to read a few more pages about alchemy. She was disappointed that her session with Marguerite that morning was too short to cover some issues that she hoped to discuss. For example, to a chemist, the word *mercury* means the element mercury; but to an alchemist, *mercury* is the spirit of the medicinal plant which could be fermented into one of the alcohols. Most interesting, since spirit and alcohol generally go hand in hand in any language. Lila's last worry before sleep was Henrietta's disappearance.

Day 2: Friday

The next morning, Lila's covers were tossed and twisted, like a wasted battle zone, so she striped the bed down to the mattress and started over. While struggling with the sheets, she remembered her bad dream about Henrietta. In some eerie and diaphanous atmosphere, Henrietta was cold, lost, and searching for a way home. There was no happy ending nor was there any ending. Lila did not put much stock into dreams like Violet could, but still, it left her with an unsettled feeling this morning.

Lila put on coffee and tea water, pulled on a jacket, and went up to the henhouse to let out the chickens and hoped that Henrietta might have found her way home. Unfortunately she counted only eight happy hens and one surly rooster looking down on her, literally and figuratively. A small thought niggled at her. Sometimes George roosted up in the loft of the bee barn. Maybe Henrietta followed him up there and was trapped somehow.

When that thought tumbled into her mind, she rushed up to the bee barn with a step stool which she needed to reach the first rung of the makeshift ladder nailed to the wall. Just as she had climbed to the top rung, she heard Violet ask, "What are you doing up there?"

"Looking for Henrietta," came her hurried reply.

"Well," Violet responded, "I can assure you, she is not up there."

Lila huffed and puffed and gave her friend a dismissive look. Violet did inherit her mother's gift of intuition and fortune-telling, but she did not have any better ideas yesterday than that they should continue on up the hill above the run. Lila took her time to have a good look around, and she found many bronze feathers; but George also has bronze feathers and he spends time up here when she lets the loft door open for him. George must have been making himself quite at home, she thought when she noticed that one of the ancient hay bales had been scratched open and strewn about, but squirrels often made nests up here also.

Breakfast over and cleanup done, they decided to drive over to Goshen to see if they could talk to Mrs. Swanson and see if she might know who owned Violet's old homestead. The house was perhaps one of the oldest structures in the county, built with solid timber construction by Violet's great-great-grandfather, Niles Stanton. The last of the Stantons had moved away twenty years ago, but Mrs. Swanson had a sharp mind and would remember Crazy Stanton. Everyone remembered him.

Before stopping to see Mrs. Swanson, Violet wanted to stop along the road with the house in sight and sort out her ambivalent feelings for the homestead and assimilate Mother Nature's partial reclamation into present reality. It had been a fine farmhouse in its day. Had good bones, as they say now. There were so many emotions battling for her attention that she could not single out one nor encapsulate any particular feeling. On the contrary, years ago Lila had spent many hours there with her good friend and had no trouble seeing it as a happy place, except for one or two minor incidences. But Lila knew that with all families, you take the bad with the good, and if you are lucky, the balance sways to the good. And she was thinking that Violet was lucky indeed!

Before scouting out the homestead, they decided to swing on up to see Mrs. Swanson and have a chat. The Swanson house still stood there, formidable and proud, perched a little higher on the hill, than several surrounding homes; and the ladies noticed that from this vantage point, the Swansons could look down on the Stantons. Even though the once-elegant Swanson home was now a little gray and tattered, one could sense that it had been majestic for its time and place. It was said to have wallpaper and flush toilets imported from France. And by peeking into windows years ago, Violet and her kid brother knew that it contained a grand piano which someone could play and play well. Violet was an able critic since she could play the piano quite well herself. How she had longed to sit down at that grand piano for just one hour instead of her clunky and ancient upright. Thank goodness her dad was good at tuning.

This Swanson home had been built by Howard Swanson, a lumber baron, back in the day when lumber was king in these parts. It was said that Howard was a self-made man, but Lila's dad knew that Howard had been given a leg up by an ambitious father who swindled many folks out of their land when they got into debt. Good timberland that is. And Howard further benefited from free transportation since he could float his logs down to a ready market by way of the Susquehanna River. But his daughter-in-law, the current Mrs. Swanson, had been a generous soul, donating much of her inheritance to worthy causes, even though she had become a recluse and preferred to keep to herself. Some thought she might be trying to get "right with God" by atoning for the sins of her husband and her father-in-law. But then again, perhaps she just wanted to look squarely into the looking glass.

Finally Mrs. Swanson came to the door with her customary suspicious gaze which softened a bit when she saw Lila. Of course, she kept her left foot in the crack of the door, even after she stepped out to see why Lila would stop twice in one week. Not customary, definitely uninvited. Lila persuaded her that she probably would remember Cliff Stanton's daughter, Violet. After dropping her eyelids into a magnifying squint, she allowed that she did. "Oh yes, and now I remember that you youngsters were the ones that peeked into my windows at night when I played the piano. Oh yes, do not deny it, young lady. And then you and your brother used to knock, run, and hide, just as I got to the door."

When Violet reacted slightly negatively to this little remonstrance, through a tensing of the shoulders, she felt Lila's right shoe briefly tap her left shoe. Realizing what Lila was relaying to her, she quickly relaxed, and with her most winning apologetic smile, she asked Mrs. Swanson for forgiveness for her childhood pranks. Mrs. Swanson also relaxed, just a tiny bit, and almost returned the smile. Lila wondered again if Violet really understood how powerful her gift was; she could have charmed Ebenezer long before the ghost arrived on the scene.

With Lila squirming to ask Mrs. Swanson if she might know who currently owned the old Stanton farm, Violet butt in to ask Mrs. Swanson if she still played the piano. "Oh my, no! I haven't touched it in years, I was never very good, and now no self-respecting tuner would come near that thing."

Through sparkling eyes, Violet and Lila shared the private joke of that Thar Thing, but they kept the smile hidden. Violet hurried on to compliment Mrs. Swanson, saying that she was worthy of playing in Carnegie Hall. Warming to the compliment, she asked Violet if she stilled played and said she remembered the warm summer evenings when the Stanton hoedowns came up on the wind. "It seems like your whole family was musically talented."

"All, except my mother," Violet replied. "She had different talents." To this response, all three exchanged knowing looks, but each held their own concept of exactly what Holly's talents had been. Mrs. Swanson gave a slight sniff, aimed down at the Stanton house, as though Holly's talents were still hovering on the breeze. Since Lila had a little firsthand knowledge with Holly's talents, she put in mind to ask Violet some questions about those gifts, later at bee time.

Finally in answer to Lila's query, Mrs. Swanson allowed that it was none of her business who might own that rundown place. So many people have come and gone, doing as little as possible until it was finally unlivable, not kept in decent shape as the Stantons used to do. It was a shame as it could have been an asset to the community, being the first working farm in the county, and now, just a standing disgrace. I do not look down that way anymore. Perhaps it would be better set to torch or torn down. Lila recoiled at this and said that Vinnie could fix and shore up just about any old structure. Then with a sudden inspiration, she wondered to herself, maybe, just maybe, Mrs. Swanson might not have given away all of her inheritance. But she realized that she was getting too far ahead of herself.

The two friends decided to drive down the short lane to the old homestead and have a close-up look. Lila shuddered when she realized that it did look abandoned and misused. It now looked even better suited for Holly's mystical talents. After sitting quietly in Doozie for ten minutes, blending current impressions with their fond memories, they decided that it did not look quite so bad. Perhaps even fixable. After all, the house was still straight up and the barn was leaning only a little toward Swansons. The back porch had caved in, but they were anxious to see if the front flagstone patio was still intact where many of their musical soirees were held on warm summer nights. Anyone could attend for a donation tossed into the hat or just stop along the road for free and roll their windows down. Violet was remembering her sister, Hyacinth, who played the washtub cello, her Bello Cello, and played it better than anyone in the county. She sure could make that thing talk and sing, keeping the beat after her drummer brother left for service in Korea. And many traveling musicians, passing through from one major city to another, would stop by for the night and join in. Violet and Hyacinth fell in love with many of the guitar players. Or was it the other way around?

Lila was never allowed to stay overnight when the Stantons hosted a traveling company. Lila's mother was a very wise woman.

Before getting out of the car, Violet leaned over and said wistfully, "Those were the days."

Lila nodded, understanding perfectly, and jumped out of the car so she could beat Violet to the porch door which, of course, was locked. They marched around the entire perimeter, peeking in windows and looking for an entry point. The music patio was still intact under a layer of sod and bramble bushes. Violet was missing Hyacinth mightily. Daddy Stanton use to hold ten-minute family prayer meetings on this patio, praying to the Lord Almighty, and Hy used to wink and whisper to Vi, "All righty, Mr. Tightie."

It was the Hy-Vi link. And their mum, in an altered state, would kneel there, with eyes closed, communicating with her ancestors or any other spirit who might be on the wing at the time. They each worshiped in their own way, probably just as most churchgoers secretly worship while the pastor waxes on with his prepared sermon. Also sitting at the back of the church, like so many do, provides too much eye fodder—too many people, men and women, forget to comb the back of their hair. These simple meetings on the patio, without too many distractions, were probably about as close to the Almighty as one could get.

After this brief reverie, the ladies continued their hunt for an unlocked door. If they had found an open door, they would have secreted on in; but they decided that breaking and entering was too unlawful. Of course, they could head on into the town hall to see if the official log books had an owner's name, but that would stir up gossip which neither wanted. If that did not work, Lila was thinking that Burt might know the owner and they could find him at Jed's tomorrow morning. But then again, Burt was the biggest broadcaster of news in the county, next to Rachel, that is. At the same time, both ladies remembered that many a night, they sneaked in and out of the house by way of the old cellar door. So as a last attempt to enter, they hurried around to the cellar entryway which was capped with metal bifold doors, held firmly in place with several inches of sod supporting the growth of a porcelain berry bush. They reasoned that this would only be entry, not as bad as breaking and entering. After wrestling with the door for several minutes, they realized that they needed better tools of the trade.

While gathering tools from Lila's tool shed, a white pickup, with orange lettering, pulled into the driveway. Violet was keen to see what Roger looked like in daylight, so she hurried down to explain that she did not need his help but really wanted to thank him for the other night. He said he wanted to give her his telephone number, just in case she needed anything. And he was free this weekend if she wanted to go with him to a bluegrass concert over in Halston. *Aha*! Lila thought, *he already knows about her musical talents*. Violet did not say yes, but she did not say no either. Lila was not keen about further contact with this Roger fellow since she wanted to light up Vinnie's interest in Violet before she had a chance to squish any bluegrass between her toes.

With shovels and tools loaded, the ladies headed back to the Goshen homestead and decided to park Doozie, sort of hidden, around the back. There was little traffic on this dirt back road to Goshen, but you never know. With the shrub, sod, and debris removed, they still needed the crowbar to lift up the metal doors with rusty hinges. Screeching and complaining, one of the bifold doors released its long-term grip on the homestead. Now looking down three cement steps, they were faced with the inner timber door which may or not be locked from the inside with a bar placed completely across the door frame. While Violet's emotions sank and she sat down on the top step, Lila tried for a few hip bumps, thinking that over the years, careless occupiers might not have bothered to bar the door. She implored Violet to help. With all hips swinging, the door did give way, fussing and groaning.

Adjusting to the stingy light admitted through two very small casement windows, they took several minutes to take in the sights, smells, and sounds found only in farmhouse basements. The spring was gently trickling as the overflow water was sluicing down the spillway trough to the underground outside spout. Not for the first time, it occurred to Lila that Violet's great-great-grand-father was the smartest homesteader in the area as he built his house directly over a water spring and had cold running water and refrigeration right downstairs in the basement. No need to send little ones outside to the springhouse for the chilled milk. Her great-great-grandmother must have been overly impressed with her very smart husband.

In more amazed wonder, the two intruders brushed off a tangle of cobwebs from the door leading into the cold storage room which had been carved into the earth, utilizing the fifty-five-degree temperature the earth provided for much of the year. Miraculously the earthen shelves still held a few labeled mason jars containing peaches, beets, and tomatoes. Violet remembered that she did like her grandmother's beet relish. Both ladies remembered how they used to sneak through the upstairs pantry, quietly lift the little black latch on the inner door, and creep down the cellar steps. With their golden prize of snatched peaches in hand, they would steal away to their playhouse for a little party. Sometimes they had to invite her little brother in but only when he caught on to the thievery. Her daddy, as she called him, had repurposed the unused henhouse for the Hy-Vi playhouse with "Hy-Vi" painted above the door. The Stantons were not home enough to keep any animals except Mutt, a large mongrel dog, who traveled everywhere with them and was also famous for singing a duet with Violet's older brother, Cliff Stanton Jr. When Stanton Jr. left home, Mutt gave up his singing career, probably due to a broken heart.

Just as they decided to start up the cellar stairs to gain entry to the first floor through the pantry, they heard a car rumbling down the rutted driveway and a car door slam. Peeking out, Lila saw a sheriff's deputy car pulling up next to Doozie. Lila told Violet to hike up her skirt just a little and put on her best innocent smile as only she could do. Lila was not good at either. They stepped outside to intercept the very young officer and say sweet hellos. He said that he was curious when he saw the red Jeep partially hidden by the empty corn crib and wondered what it was doing there. Violet explained that this had been her family home for many years and they were just wandering down memory lane.

Well, the officer was extremely young and soberly intent on doing his duty and also immune to Violet's famous smile and shapely calves. He suggested that they were trespassing and that they needed an official letter of approval from the owners to see the inside. They agreed to talk with an official at town hall in Alma. He gave the ladies an escort out the lane and watched until they headed on into Alma to talk to a clerk. Violet murmured, "Mr. Deputy was wearing his whitey tighties too tight." Knowing that Violet would write a new song about Mr. Deputy, Lila chuckled all the way to town,

At town hall, they did find out the owner's name, Zack Williams, and last known address and that he owed back taxes of $500. The ladies decided to not stir up too much notice in their interest and the clerk seemed to care even less, so they took their info and slipped out the door. They decided to return to Lila's for now.

Over wine, they could plan a strategy. Vinnie was just returning from the jobsite and slowed to a stop, rolled down his window to say hello as they were pulling into the Lilaland. They asked him if he knew this Williams fellow, and he nodded a hesitant yes. He understood that said Williams was a no-account bloke who had lived in Violet's homestead for several years with various friends, refusing to make repairs, and moved out after it was completely unlivable. He declined the invitation to join them for wine which was just as well since Lila wanted to get Violet excited to buy the farm, maybe now for just back taxes, before she got Vinnie excited about repairs. But she did notice that Vinnie did take an extra moment to take in Violet's electric smile.

With a casserole on low in the oven, they headed on up to the bee barn. Lila had refurbished the inside of this little barn soon after she returned. After she had the beehives installed into the side of the barn, she scrubbed, painted walls, hung paintings, and repurposed flea market cabinets to house bee tools and shelves to hold her bee books. She decided to use artfully stacked hay bales and cover them with colorful afghan throws for seating and hung antique rustic chandeliers for lighting. It was a delight, and Lila often enjoyed a relaxing moment inside the barn. And she had a stethoscope to listen for activity inside the hive, giving her a metric for colony conditions. Since Violet would not be afraid of a little guard bee peeking out the back of the hive into the barn, the two ladies decided on this chilly evening to have their wine inside the bee barn. But strangely, Benny hung back and could not be coaxed into the barn. Instead he laid his head on the open threshold so he could hear the chatter but kept his body to the outside.

It was decided that first thing tomorrow morning, they would haul planks up to the run to do some staging for the bridge construction. After that, they would pack some sandwiches and take with them over to the old homestead. They discussed hiding the Jeep further behind the barn, just in case Mr. Whitey Tightie was out cruising, and Violet was practically euphoric about getting into the Hy-Vi bedroom. Many years ago, she hid her childhood attempts at song writing from prying eyes in the back of a dresser and wanted to see if the musical scores were still there. Her son, who was now well established in the music publishing business, wanted them as keepsakes. On the other hand, Lila had different interests and was anxious to see the ancestor parlor and wanted to know how Holly called Uncle Roland back from the heavenly beyond. As a child, this was all scary and believable, even though her wise mother told her it was all trickery. Violet laughed and said that she would expose her charlatan mother tomorrow. "You know, Mother had quite a following, and she made her pocket money with her trade. Dad was not very good at holding onto his money."

On the way back down the cosmos path to the house, they veered over to the chicken yard to round up the hens for the night. No Henrietta, and Lila had started to accept that she would not be there.

Before retiring for the night, Violet suggested that they should check with Dave tomorrow to find out the status of repairs. *Maybe*, thought Lila, *Dave might convince Vi to trade that Thar Thing on a good used car.*

Lila read *Art of Alchemy* well into the night and made some notations that she wanted to discuss with Marguerite. After all, Jed was convinced that Marguerite's medicine saved his grandson's life after the doctors had failed. Lila knew, with time, she could gain Marguerite's confidence and trust if she proceeded slowly with some actual knowledge of her elixir art. Also just from personal interest, she wanted to learn a little more about the Nutmeg Wars and the tiny island where nutmeg was first discovered. After all what would pumpkin pie taste like if we had no nutmeg? And what can nutmeg do for your health?

Before turning out the light, Lila reviewed some of Jed's concerns about Marguerite who he believed was an answer to a prayer. On his first trip there, he found a well-maintained homesteader cabin which was attached, in the back, to a larger building with several exhaust stacks, one peeking from the side and one from the top. The property was better maintained than Jed had expected based on hearsay. There were well-tended plots of plants, cordoned off into ten-foot squares. This all probably dated back to her grandfather who was known for extracting medicinal plants ages ago.

Recently, he made a trip back to the Hollow, hoping to get more of the plant elixir for his grandson. As before, Jed was greeted by the very large mastiff guard dog who was not happy to have company. He sat in his truck and waited until he noticed a moving shadow cross a curtained window in the back. And so, he waited for a spell—what seemed forever—but when the shadow crossed again, he decided to roll down the window and wave as he had done on his first trip, hoping to send a friendly signal, but the mastiff misinterpreted his intentions and lunged angrily at the truck. Jed got the window rolled up just before man and dog collided face-to-face. Just as he was about to leave, a door on the back of the larger addition opened slightly and the mastiff responded to a little whistle and bounded into the building. Jed decided that he was safe for now and could afford to be patient.

Finally the small cabin door opened and Marguerite cautiously stuck her head out with a questioning expression. Jed yelled, "Marguerite, it's me, Jed. I need more medicine for my grandson."

Marguerite shook her head and said, "I gave you all. The alembic broke. Can't make more."

Jed yelled back, "Let me help, I know a woman recently retired from chemistry. She would know how to get you set up again."

Marguerite said she would think about it and firmly closed her door. Quietly sitting there and thinking, Jed knew it would take some collaboration with Lila and a few more rounds with the mastiff before he gained Marguerite's confidence. Pondering on all this, Lila dropped off to sleep with the book open and the light still on.

Day 3: Saturday

Violet woke first and went down to start Lila's coffee and fire up the tea water. She was anxious for the day to begin as there was much on the plate for today. She was excited to talk to Dave but knew that they were going to start on the bridge construction first. She wanted to get Lila moving. Lila came cautiously down the stairs, carefully negotiating the funny little curve and found Vi making toast with honey and peanut butter topping. No, Vi did not want eggs this morning, so they ate and drank their meager breakfast before setting off with Doozie for bridge construction over Alder Run. It was still chilly, so they were dressed in waterproof boots and warm jackets. Alder Run, full of itself this morning, was talking and babbling. Benny jumped in and was chasing some foam spewed up by a little dam of sticks and leaf debris, making the ladies laugh.

The foundation stones, installed earlier, still held true and tight, so the ladies pushed, prodded, and pounded the sturdy planks into place while the cold water crashed at their ankles. The bridge was good enough for now but looked unfinished. She would talk with Vinnie about some railings sometime in the future, especially if he had a good harvest from her sugar maple trees. Violet thought Lila should take the virginal trip across the new bridge, but Lila insisted that they should start at opposite ends and meet in the middle, just like on their bicycles years ago. They saluted high fives when they met and renewed their promise to always be there for each other. Before they left, Violet said she had a feeling that on another day, they should search the hillside, up through the maples, for evidence of Henrietta. "No," Lila said pensively, "I have made my peace. It is time to let her go."

With sandwiches and lemonade packed into a picnic basket, they headed out for the day. They stopped at Dave's to get the bad news that the parts he needed had not arrived yet. Clearly Violet was now quite agitated and worried about getting back for her medical appointments. Cautiously Lila let this problem rest until Vi was ready to tell her about it, but she thought maybe she already knew. Lila had no Clairvoyant talents like Violet possessed, but she noticed that Vi often touched her left breast. But that could also imply cardiac problems as well.

As they turned the car left, off the main route 5, onto the hard pack Goshen road, excitement escalated. On the approach to the hamlet, they glanced up to Swanson Hill where they noticed a service van parked in the driveway. Curious, they drove slowly on past to read the lettering on the van—Harper's Piano Tuning. Wide eyed, Violet sang out, "There's a thaw on the hill," to the tune of "Go Tell It on the Mountain." She played the dashboard like a piano and stomped her feet like a drum until she had Lila pumping the gas feed and singing along, "In Goshen, the Piano Man cometh."

After turning around at the next crossroads, they slipped on past Swanson's and drove down the Stanton lane and hid Doozie behind the barn. With combined courage, they raced to the house. Lila won, as always. Violet had longer legs, but Lila had the stronger desire to win. They entered through the basement, raced up the stairs, and stepped into the pantry. Both stopped for a breath. Lila hung back in the pantry, allowing Violet the privilege to enter the kitchen first. As she waited and glanced around, she noticed another exit door covered with a curtain which must open into the ancestor parlor. Lila never realized that door ever existed. Just then, she heard a small "oh" escape from Violet.

As Lila stepped into the silence of the once-bustling kitchen, she realized that the hum she was hearing was coming from her own body. She wondered if Violet's gift of seeing was engaged. Watching Violet trail her hand over the once-beautiful Hoosier cabinet, now weighed down with many coats of ugly paint, Lila was hopeful that there may still be some other Stanton furniture that was not sold, burned, or trashed. Sadly, however, the large family table and chairs were gone and Grandma's rocking chair was missing. At the kitchen sink window, Violet pulled back the decayed lace curtain only to have it disintegrate into powder. They each took their time adjusting to their own expectation. Reality itself is bent by space-time and the memory of it is bent even further. But right here, right now, Violet was standing in a new moment, in the essence of the thing, finding it difficult to reconcile the memory with the moment. They started out in a whisper so as not to disturb—who knew what? Maybe Violet knew, but Lila was not blessed, or cursed, with the gift.

On their way to the stairs, they glanced into the music parlor, but Violet was anxious to see her old bedroom, also dreading that she would not find her manuscripts. The Hy-Vi bedroom held out some promise of anchoring Vi to the idea of returning home again, so Lila did not push to see the music or the ancestor parlor. Out of habit, Violet skipped the fifth stair, but curious Lila wanted to make sure that it still squeaked, and it did. Holly always wanted it fixed, but Daddy Stanton said that it is was a good thing when you are raising teenagers or listening for burglars. However, all the Stanton children knew to skip the fifth stair when sneaking in late. They would warn each other, "Don't forget the fifth." The first time Lila heard that, she thought these musical siblings were talking about Beethoven.

Violet's heart was palpitating as she entered her bedroom. So many years here with her sister, so many things she yearned to tell her. Quietly Lila stepped back out of the room to give Violet some time but not before she noticed that the birds-eye maple bedroom furniture was gone. Gone! The only furniture left was their built-in hope chest wedged into the windowed alcove, overlooking the patio. Hy and Vi had the best view from here as they watched for company driving into the yard below. To give the girls the best bedroom was such a generous thing. Lila wandered into the other bedrooms which were rooms that were never familiar to her. She found them full of potential and could easily imagine them remodeled and decorated with appropriate farmhouse furniture. The bathroom was spacious but would need a total overhaul. Perhaps the claw-foot tub could be kept for effect. Funny thing, why was the commode missing? Who takes the commode with them when they move?

Peeking into Violet's bedroom, she could see her sitting on the floor next to the opened hope chest and reading a small book, so she slipped back downstairs and stopped by the small room that the Stantons called the music equipment room. Years ago, this room was always filled with musical stuff, in various states of repair. Daddy Stanton made a little money fixing and inventing musical instruments. Now it was only stuffed with stuff. *Well,* she thought, *Violet could sort this all out when she gets ownership.* But something caught Lila's eye over in the far dark corner—the Bello-Cello, a.k.a. Hyacinth's washtub minus the mop handle with horse hair strings. With this discovery, she got so excited that she thought she had to pee; but there was no running water now. In fact, there wasn't even a commode. She wondered if she should risk running out behind the barn, but the urge passed as she went across the hall into the music parlor, where many musicals and practices were held, especially in inclement weather.

Not too much to see in here, furniture either taken by Stantons or other renters and inhabitants. Even Violet's large upright piano was gone. Stantons did not have room in the van when they moved South to live in Gatlinburg, so they left it behind. It was ether taken or chopped up for firewood by renters. The only piece of furniture left was Grandma Stanton's antique Singer sewing machine, and Lila remembered how Grandma Stanton could make that Singer sing. In fact, Violet and Hyacinth were always the best-dressed little girls in grade school. With lace and bric-a-brac, Grandma could even make their flour sack dresses look like they came from Shanebrooks Department Store in Alma. All the girls were a little envious, except Hildegarde, who did buy her clothes from Shanebrooks.

Waiting for Violet, Lila peaked into the ancestor parlor, which was directly behind the music parlor, but Lila wanted to wait for Vi before opening the bifold glass doors. These doors were pretty grand for a farmhouse. Once again great-great-grandma must have been proud of her clever husband. Scanning the room, she saw some remnants of the velvet curtains which were used to darken the room when Holly held ancestor sessions. Over in the far corner, she noticed a metal exhaust furnace pipe which seemed to stretch from the floor all the way up into Violet's bedroom. There was a rod at the top which must have held a concealing curtain at some time in the past. *Odd,* she thought as she knew that years ago, the heat radiated up from the first floor to the second floor through registers which one could close and open at will. Vi's bedroom was always a little frosty. Well, perhaps new owners had installed central heating, but she doubted that. Then she suddenly remembered the extra door which she had noticed while in the pantry. Quickly she glanced over to that corner. Sure enough, there it was!

Still waiting for Violet, Lila went over to look out the front door which led out to the music patio; she heard Violet coming into the room with two small books in her hand. She was smiling but it looked like she had been crying. Hesitantly Lila asked if the books contained her music scores. "No, no music scores, but I did find our diaries," which she held up triumphantly. "You won't believe some of the things we wrote back then. I will read some of the better parts to you while we have our sandwiches out on the patio."

After the last crumbs were wolfed down and the diaries read, Lila said it was time to open up the ancestor parlor. She could not wait to see how her adult self would react to this room that had been wrapped in so much mystery. Her first real experience there had been for a tea-leaf reading by Holly. She had coaxed her mother to go as other girlfriends had gone and were having such fun at school describing them. These tea parties were held in the ancestor parlor, around a table set with fine linens and bone china teacups. Loose tea was steeped for an exact number of minutes, and then was poured into the cups in such a way as to allow a few leaves to fall to the bottom of the cup. After the tea was carefully sipped, the leaves formed a pattern on the bottom of the cup with which only Holly could read your future based on your pattern.

Finally her mother agreed, but only if she and other mothers all agreed to go together. And she warned Lila that this was all just silly make-believe stuff and a frightful waste of two dollars per person. Well, they did go, in fancy dresses and shoes, and Lila, at age ten, learned that her tea leaves foretold that she was going to go on to a fine college someday and marry a handsome fellow by the name of Harry or was it Larry? And the mothers, including Lila's, all had such a hilarious time that they agreed to do it again some time, money be damned. Obviously Holly had a gift of something.

Lila remembered that she was twelve years of age before was allowed to attend a real seeing. Somehow she convinced her mother that she could go with Aunt Sue and her daughter, Bonnie. Aunt Sue wanted to call in dear departed Uncle Roland, a longtime reverend at the Evangelical United Brethren Church. It seemed that she had some unresolved issues with her saintly uncle. Steadfast in his evangelist calling, he believed true baptism could only be accomplished by full immersion in the Susquehanna River. Aunt Sue happened to have the only cleared road access to the river due to some previous timbering on her property. The river was a good two miles off of the main highway and being a logging road, it was rough and rutted. At first, the arrangement to travel past her house was free, but as these baptism events gained huge popularity with a picnic-like atmosphere, hundreds came down her road for a day's outing. As time went on, she renegotiated with Uncle Roland that he would charge a fee for each buggy that used her road for these events. Well, he may have charged the fee but Aunt Sue never saw a dime.

To young Lila, it was all frightfully scary, even before Uncle Roland's spirit was called down. As the flickering candles and ethereal music was setting the mood, Madame Holly swished into the darkened parlor, dressed in a lace mantilla and a black crepe dress, weighed down with five strands of purple and silver beads. Madame Holly went through a lot of gyrations and chanting before settling into a trance and talking to her crystal ball.

Lila remembered that the crystal ball on the black table did some sparking and sputtering in response to Madame's voice. Then when Uncle's spirit floated into the room, along with some faint perfumery odor, the ball got really excited. Oh yes, he could communicate responding to requests by making strange distant noises. One twang for yes, two twangs for no, and a door creaking for I don't know. All Lila could remember was that Aunt Sue seemed to be very distressed with Uncle Roland's answers since he responded mostly with door creaking but very little twanging. After uncle was bored with the whole affair, he flew away somewhere. Madame explained that sometimes, the spirits need more time to think things over and perhaps he would be more forthcoming on the next visit. Aunt Sue doubted that there would be a next visit, but she paid Madame some money. Regretfully Lila still could not recall how much this seeing had cost, but she thought it likely that Holly was seriously underpaid for this wonderful stage performance—worthy of a Sarah Bernhardt masterpiece theater production. And now, standing here as an adult, where this adventure took place, she thought how ingenious Holly had been. Such a talent, unrecognized by us all.

With her hand on the tarnished brass handle of the bifold doors, Violet looked at Lila and said, "I am ready if you are." Of course, Lila had been ready for quite some time. Each pushed a door open and stepped into the room, the room which had always been off-limits to them unless Holly herself gave permission. As they hesitated, searching for their bearings, it felt a little like forbidden company fruit. Violet tried to see the room as it once was, and Lila tried to see the room as it looked now.

"Okay, girlfriend," Violet coaxed. "What do you want to know?"

"Well," answered Lila, "I have already worked out the door-creaking sounds," as she pointed to the recently discovered door over in the corner, "but which one of you pushed on the door for the I-don't-know response?"

Violet smiled playfully. "That would have been one of the boys hiding back in the pantry."

"That explains the creaking, but how did the essence of lavender flood the room just as the spirit was called down?"

"That was a clever addition worked out by the boys. They warmed up the perfume on a hot plate and sprayed it under the door with Mum's perfume atomizers. They timed it by listening to cues in Mum's voice."

"Okay, I get that, but what I haven't worked out yet was the twanging for yes or no."

Mischievously Violet pulled a juice harp out of her pocket which she found upstairs, tucked away in the hope chest along with her diaries, and Lila was thunderstruck. Of course, both girls could make the juice harp talk. Violet proceeded to twang a yes and a no, only to make Lila laugh so hard now that she really had to pee and soon. But not before Violet ran back upstairs to her bedroom, threw back the rug, and leaned into the metal pipe and twanged—"Oh-oh, hello, Lila." Lila was laughing all the way to the barn.

Back home, Lila convinced Vi to take the first shower while she ran up to the henhouse. Benny helped with rounding up the hens and then coaxed to go on up to the bee barn. Lila decided it wouldn't hurt to make sure the barn door was closed for the night. It was. She peeked anyway. All looked okay and Benny, doing his duty, ran around the barn, sniffing for tracks and scents. "Come along, Benny, Violet and I have an important dinner date." She knew they were running a little late and she did not want to keep Vinnie waiting.

Violet came downstairs in a lovely soft powder-blue dress which complimented her eyes, hair, and most of all, her figure. Not to mention the well-chosen jewelry. All at once, Lila wished that she had taken the time at Shanebrooks the other day to update her tired wardrobe. But nothing to be done for it now. After all, it wasn't as if they were going over to Ophelia's in Alma. Since she came back home, there was not too much need for party clothes.

They were ten minutes late arriving at Michael's and Vinnie was already seated. Always the gentleman, he rose and gave each lady a compliment. Their table was in the far corner and it seemed very private, even though the place was packed. Over drinks, the ladies recounted their day at the homestead, skipping the part about Vinnie being mentioned several times in Violet's diary. It took no time at all to have Vinnie chortling about their visit to the ancestor parlor. He said that his mother had attended a seeing years ago and she thought it was a hoax but was not entirely sure. He remembered that his dad was quite unhappy when he heard how much it had cost. Vinnie thought the part about the juice harp twanging and the door creaking was hilarious. And he allowed that his mother probably got more than her money's worth.

But there was still something Lila wanted explained. How did the crystal ball flash and flutter? With a proud smile, Violet said "Well, you know, Daddy was always handy and clever. He placed several strings of Christmas lights into the globe and ran the cord down through a hole in the table. This was hooked into a connection under the table with a circuit breaker interrupter so that Mum could operate the whole contraption with a foot pedal and call down the spirits. The mere mention of circuit breakers was Vinnie's chance to shine. He used up twenty minutes on how easily the flashing could be accomplished, even orchestrating one color string alternately with one white string. Yes, Cliff and Vinnie would have been a deliciously dangerous pair in the ancestor room.

Over dinner, Lila gently brought up that fact that she was hoping that Violet might consider buying and rehabilitating the old homestead. In its present condition, it could be purchased rather cheaply; and with the right construction know-how, it could be put back into a working farm and a real landmark, being perhaps the first farm in the county. Vinnie looked at Violet. Violet looked at Lila. Lila looked at Vinnie. All went silent. Lila was afraid that she had put a damper on the good mood, but she forged ahead, now that her thoughts made the journey to the table. She was careful not to mention about the back taxes. She did not want to have Vinnie jump in to buy the place for a turnaround sale. But he was the only one she trusted to help Violet with rehabbing the house.

Vinnie broke the silence by asking about the condition of the interior. Judging by the exterior, he said that it looked to be in poor shape. But Lila reassured him that it was not beyond fixing. Since she peaked under the old carpets, she knew the hardwood floors were still in excellent shape, there were no sagging ceilings anywhere, there were several broken windows, but the sills were not yet rotted. She was sure central heating, total rewiring, and replumbing could be accomplished with his help. Normally loquacious, Violet was now speechless. Vinnie is looking skeptically at Lila over the top of his glasses. Seeing how serious she was, he smiled and said, "If it is going to be a restoration, who will locate the old commode?" That certainly lightened the mood, and over coffee, they made small talk and said they would try to get together again before Violet left.

Lila had trouble getting to sleep that night, thinking about Holly's two gifts: the ability to act and the ability to see backward and forward. Sure, much of it was pure intuition, aided by a little fakery, but still, might it not be possible to look both ways if time is a continuum in the space-time fabric as Einstein intuits? Two sides of the same coin, so to speak. In other words, once you take the time to think *right now*, that moment is already in the past, and my now-time would not be your now-time. Maybe there simply is no *now*. She wanted to ask Violet what her take was on Holly's ability to forecast events. They had so much more to discuss.

Day 4: Sunday

Over breakfast, they discussed how fun dinner was last night and they were still chuckling about Vinnie's interest in the ancestor parlor. They steered away from the subject of purchasing the homestead. Violet mentioned that she might want to get grandmother's sewing machine out of the house. But Lila was thinking that if Violet purchased the house, then they should leave it right there. And then there was the issue of all that stuff in the music storage room, plus Hyacinth's Bello-Cello. Lila wondered if Violet's music scores might be in there, but Vi was very doubtful about that. She was sure they went with the birds-eye maple dresser, wherever that might be.

Then Lila suggested that since it was Sunday that they take a break today, skip church, pack a snack, and hike up to Caleb's Lookout. This would give them some alone time for sharing plans and hopes for the future. Years ago, the summit of Crescent Ridge was a gentle climb for them; but now, it would be a good workout. Benny loved the climb. The lookout at the top afforded views into two valleys, one to the east and one to the west. The weather promised to be good. And yes, as promised, Violet brought hiking clothes. Noticing that Violet did not hesitate, Lila eliminated cardiac trouble. Violet had the gift of forecasting, but Lila had the gift of discerning.

Then they wondered when they should check on Mrs. Swanson. Violet said it would be such a thrill just to sit at that grand piano and imagine she was a child again. Lila suggested that they could stop by tomorrow while in Goshen; they still wanted to tour the barn and check on the lower meadow at Vi's homestead. "Perhaps we can come up with a good excuse for stopping."

Lila figured that they could just tell Mrs. Swanson that they were researching the history of the old homestead and thought she would know many details. Violet warmed to this idea.

The day started out cool and overcast, perfect for hiking. Halfway up, they stopped for a sip of water and sat comfortably on a large stone which had many initials and dates carved into it. They recognized most of them. Then an older couple, probably in their middle to late sixties, whizzed past them with their walking sticks a-clacking and a-digging. They waved but kept moving. Benny jumped up, urging his charges to get a move on, so they laughingly trudged on up the hill behind him. From time to time, he circled back down around, snuffing encouragement. Before they reached the top, the older couple came fast, stepping back down, and reported, "Cloudy day, can't see naught." And they continued down faster than going up.

Right on cue, a warm sun broke through the clouds just as they reached the top, giving them a beautiful view out over Goshen to the west and over Hastings to the east. They spent twenty minutes reviewing all the landmarks. The old fire tower was still there on the opposite hilltop. Down in the valley of rolling hills, Violet's homestead was hidden by trees, but they could make out the Swanson house. Lila knew this was a poignant moment since Violet's eyes looked a little misty. She had a wonderful childhood in that valley, and no doubt, many hidden memories were flooding to the fore. Lila was patient and gave her time to put memory into word. As the clouds were winging by, Violet remembered that Old Caleb had said that up here, the clouds carried the stamp of heaven. Pausing to digest this statement, Lila felt that she was sniffing the air of infinity, and yes, she guessed, that would be big enough to encompass heaven.

As they munched homemade trail mix and drank raspberry water, Lila wondered out loud about Holly's forecasting ability. Violet assured Lila that her mum had an incredible ability to foresee many events.

"You know," Violet said, "she foretold the assassination of President Kennedy, including the month, even though she missed on the location. She predicted Nevada rather than Texas."

"Yes," replied Lila, "and as I remember, she also predicted that the Russians would beat everyone into space."

Violet agreed. "It is amazing once you realize that Mum never read anything except *The Grit* which came only once a week. It was spooky at times, living with her, but she was a devoted mother and certainly loved Daddy and supported all of his schemes, well, almost all." To which they had to chuckle.

"At times," Lila mused, "I sense that you inherited the gift."

Violet shook her head. "No, no, I am just good at guessing."

Lila responded with a still silence, looking off into the distance, remembering otherwise while she guessed that Violet felt pressure to not be labeled as a mystic or seer and perhaps be hobbled by expectations.

Lila wondered, *Was Holly happy after they had moved to Gatlinburg? She had such a presence about herself, she changed the atmosphere of each room she entered. I often felt she could cause a tsunami in Japan just by waving hello in Goshen.* Violet said that her mum was happy for her daddy as he was among so many gifted musicians and artists there and was having the time of his life. "Mum went along for his sake but never got her esprit back, giving up all seeing and forecasting. She did not make new friends easily. There were some likeminded folks over in the cove, but she did not reach out to them. If Daddy had died before her, then I might have considered bringing her back here to her roots, but he outlived her by two years. And then, Daddy lost his spark after Mum died."

A momentary sadness came over Lila, but she shook it off. She forged ahead to ask Violet if she could see herself ever coming back home either permanently or for vacations. Especially if they could get the farm back for her. Violet started hesitantly. "Now that my son is doing so well in Nashville and I do get to visit with him frequently, I probably will stay in the South. I have become accustomed to the climate and the people."

Still forging ahead, she asked Violet if there might not be a smoldering spark that could rekindle her old relationship with Vinnie. Violet thought that there had been too many lost chances to ever bring it to fruition. Besides he would never move South, and she did not see herself moving North. This was not the answer Lila had hoped for, but there it was. They moved on to brighter moments in their childhood past and let that subject drop for now. But then again, the week was not over yet.

Before gathering up their jackets and drinks, they took another look at the magnificent view and thought that they should have remembered binoculars. As they looked over Goshen, Violet wondered if Mrs. Swanson was practicing the piano right now. "No," Lila said, "this is her nap time."

On the way back to Lila's, Jed's Café came into view, and the open sign was still on, even though it was near the 2:00-p.m. closing time. Lila told Vi that they would stop just for a moment as Jed asked her to come during slow hours so they could discuss Marguerite. Jed must have seen them pull in because he had two cups of coffee poured, probably the last of the pot, and signaled them to come up near the counter. He turned the open sign around to closed and several curious customers slowly angled up to pay their bill. They got the message, so they finished up their sips and left. Jed said that the three of them could talk while he cleaned the grill and washed the coffeepot.

Settling in with her coffee, Lila asked," Jed, do you remember Violet from school?"

"Yes, I do. I believe you were Stanton Jr.'s kid sister. You were several years younger, probably in my sister's grade."

"Beverly," Lila guessed as Beverly was one year younger than Vi, but with Violet's intermittent schooling, she had spent some time in Beverly's grade. In fact, Violet spent a little time in nearly everyone's grade because the teachers were always confounded about her grade level.

Lila mentioned their hike up to the lookout and that they found Jed's initials on the sitting rock which made him chuckle. Jed said they camped many times at the top, but he had not been back up in years. In quiet reverie, Violet said, "I had forgotten how lovely it is up there."

Jed poured himself the last cup before putting the pot to soak and came around the counter to sit with the ladies. He inquired about Violet's family and wanted to know what ever happened to Stanton Jr. Sadly, Violet told him she did not know. After he came back from Korea, he just quietly disappeared and broke Mother's heart. "Mother believed that he got hooked on some pain killers during his rehabilitation and died in his sleep. My sister, Hyacinth, died several years ago in childbirth with diabetes complications, but little Jimmy is doing well in machine manufacturing and has several patents on his inventions. He inherited the lion's share of Daddy's talents. He is so busy that we don't get together much."

But most of all, Jed wanted to know if her father ever did get a Piper Cub or any over flying device. "Well, not exactly," she answered. "He did take up soaring lessons but that did not last long, mostly because they were too expensive. You know President Jackson and Mr. Hamilton never rubbed elbows in Daddy's wallet." Jed chuckled, remembering Cliff was long on talent but always short on money. "But Daddy was happy. After we moved to Gatlinburg, he got very involved with a popular musical group which took up a lot of his time playing at various events. It was a five-piece band which was much in demand at all the social occasions. Therefore, he could play with adults instead of whipping us four kids into shape, all the while repairing and tuning our instruments.

"Then came the big event which really cured him of the desire to fly. His friend Barry had a small airplane and had promised Daddy that he would take him up one day and show him the ropes. Well, the day came when Barry accepted an engagement for himself and Daddy to play at a big reception in Dayton, Ohio. They planned to fly up, play the event that night, and fly back the next day. You know, Mum was usually supportive of Daddy's schemes and escapades, but this time, she threw a five-star melodramatic fit, saying she was 'seeing' impending disaster here. Daddy was too excited and bent on taking the trip that he ignored her forecasting as just general worrying. The day started out calm and the weather was supposed to be good along the Great Lakes corridor for the next few days.

"The flight was going well, and Barry even let Daddy handle the controls for a little while. But as they reached the outskirts of Dayton, they ran into fog which turned so dense that it hindered any sight of land. Now if you have ever lived under the umbrella of one of the Great Lakes, then you know about fog, and sometimes even dense fog. People who live there fight off depression more often than skin cancer. Finally it became obvious that Barry was lost and did not have sophisticated automatic controls. Barry was frightened, although pretended not to be, and Daddy was praying to the Almighty as only he could do. If God would see them through this fog, he would donate half of his wages to the Good Samaritan Fund. Of course, his wages never amounted to much, but it is not the size of the gift but the intent of the gift that matters to the Almighty. Fortunately God must have been listening because the fog lifted, and they could now see Lake Erie in the distance. In the murky stew, they had overshot. Barry had to turn the airplane back south toward Dayton.

"Daddy then asked Barry if the gas gauge was accurate because he noticed that it was registering near empty. In a fit of anxious sweat, Barry said, 'Tighten up, we are going to have to set this craft down.' Luckily they were over some vineyards, not as good as a wheat field where Barry had to set one down in the past but this would have to do. Well, the plane was damaged, salvageable only for parts, but amazingly, both men walked away with only severe bruises and massive headaches. After he came slinking back home, Mum forgot all the scolding she had planned and said simply, 'Your shirt is buttoned-up wrong.' And now, they are both gone, but as they say, we have the memories."

Jed then asked Violet if she was planning to return to this area, now that most of her family was gone or missing. He proudly told her that Rockton was a very active supportive community and, "We are happy that Lila has returned. We are hoping that she will make it permanent."

Violet looked pensive and doubtful, but she told Jed that she would think about it. It occurred to Lila that Jed should be paid by the chamber of commerce for his promotion of all things good about Rockton.

At this lull in the conversation, Jed turned to Lila and asked, "Are you and Marguerite making any progress?"

"Well yes, slow to be sure, but she is learning a little chemistry and I, in turn, a little alchemy. I know I could help her with the speed and accuracy of her distillations, but first, I have to gain her trust before she will allow me to see the equipment."

"Yes," Jed replied, "I have never been inside the house myself, so I know how protective she is, not to mention her guard dog. It might help if we could get the dog's name."

Violet offered, "I am good with dogs. I should go with Lila on her first trip there."

"Thank you for the offer, but I am not ready yet to push Marguerite for the initial visit."

Violet wanted to know a little more on what kind of distillations Marguerite was doing, and Jed briefly told her that she made medical tonics from plant extracts and how she helped his grandson.

"No way!" Violet said. "You two can't be serious."

Jed said, "Oh, but I am."

"You mean after all the mockery my mother suffered from non-believers in this community, you are going to believe someone who claims she can turn mercury into gold?"

Lila replied soothingly, "Violet, I don't think Marguerite dabbles into that kind of alchemy. And alternative medicine is making quite a comeback these days, especially with those who have gone to their doctor but did not get relief."

Jed added, "And after all, many pharmaceutical companies these days are preparing medicines which have been derived from plant extracts."

"But where is the guarantee of purity and safety…the clinical trials?" Violet asked.

"Yes, Violet," Lila responded, "I see your point."

Jed said, "You are forgetting about the multitude of dangerous side effects that are endured by the so-called approved medicines."

Lowering her voice, Lila said, "I believe that it was Paracelsus who said that the 'poison was in the dose,' and I have experienced the truth of that when the doctors will give the same dosage to a one-hundred-pound woman that they give to a two-hundred-pound man."

Violet, raising her voice, said, "But that is the doctor's fault."

Lila retorted, "But when I analyzed some of the patient sampling in drug trial tests, I have noticed that sometimes, the drug companies do not take into account the patient's weight, and sometimes, the tests are flawed by excluding women from the sample pool altogether. They have found that including women in the trials makes too much variability in the results."

Raising the ante, Jed added, "And I think there are millions of wastes in the health care drug-promoted system."

Violet was nearly shouting now. "It costs the drug companies millions to make safe and effective drugs."

Jed and Violet both had their own personal bias for their line of thinking. No one comes into a discussion standing on neutral ground. Jed was molded by his previous distrust of the medical system, and Violet was molded by her distrust of quackery. Lila attempted to bring the conversation to a comfortable closure. But Jed, with his successful career of café boss and argument arbitrator, especially between Burt and Sonny, decided to tell an oft' repeated joke.

"An African tribesman went to the local medicine man to be treated for a stomach ailment. The medicine man gave him a thirty-inch leather thong, told him to eat an inch off the thong each day, and come back in thirty days. When he went back after thirty days, the medicine man asked him how he was feeling. The tribesman said, 'Not so good, the thong is gone but the malady lingers on.'"

When the two arrived back home, Lila suggested that they have an iced tea on the patio while supper was warming. She had hoped to have some quiet time to convince Violet that she might be happy here and she could preserve her family's legacy by keeping and restoring the homestead. Maybe now that her son was well-established in the music business, he might want to help. And didn't Violet mention to Jed that her brother, little Jimmy, was doing very well in manufacturing with patents to his name? He probably had a little expendable cash to honor the Stanton name.

However, Vinnie stopped in on his way home, something he was never in the habit of doing. *Progress*, Lila thought. After setting out the tea, she excused herself to round up the hens and check on the bee barn. Benny was overeager for a run since he had waited in the car while they talked with Jed. At the hen yard, Lila noticed that in Henrietta's absence, a new pecking order was established. Bridgette was now the boss, well, after George that is. Bridgette was not a beauty like Henrietta, but what a producer—never missed a day. Lila replenished their water and grit even though in these parts, there was plenty of natural grit in the ground. Benny raced Lila up to the bee barn and was sniffing and then marking his scent on the back corners. Then he scratched and sniffed some more and coaxed to go on up to the run. Lila did not oblige him, so he sulked as he came back down with her.

Entering in on the patio conversation, Lila sensed that it was only pleasant reminiscent chatter. So she was surprised when Vinnie suddenly said that he had stopped at the homestead and not only that, he also looked up some records at Alma Town Hall. Laughingly he said that he had a sterling reputation with the clerks there. *I'll bet*, thought Violet as she remembered that cute clerk they saw there. Vinnie went on to say that there might be some merit in purchasing the property, especially if it could be bought for back taxes, not something Lila wanted him to know just yet, but he was bound to find out sooner or later. There really are very few secrets hidden from the local builders. It has always been said around here that Vinnie was one of the best for getting stuff done, and he occasionally prefers to pay the fine rather than go through bureaucratic red tape to get the permit. Still he would be Lila's choice for helping Violet restore the homestead.

Vinnie continued to describe the changes they would have to make, first to bring it up to code, and secondly, to make it comfortable and livable; and as soon as he could get inside, he would know how extensive the repairs should be. Lila told him they were planning to stop there tomorrow in case he was free. Excitedly Lila slipped in what she thought would be needed, such as solarium for flowers when the back porch was rebuilt. She knew the morning sun came flashing in on that side. During this exchange, Violet remained silent but she was listening and thinking. Lila thought that Vinnie might be warming to the total package. He agreed to stay for a quick leftover dinner, even though Lila warned him that it would be vegetarian fare.

Over dinner, Vinnie told them about the new kitchen he was installing over in Alma for an eighty-year-old woman who just lost her husband. During their sixty years of marriage, he would not let her change one item in that kitchen since it had been in his family forever. Well, now she hopes that all the spirits are mightily disturbed because she purchased top-of-the-line appliances, plus a fancy coffee machine which even grinds the beans and get this—she doesn't even like coffee.

As Lila climbed into bed with her book, Violet knocked lightly, came in to say that she still thought it a good idea to get her grandmother's sewing machine out of the house because one never knows how these situations will play out. She also wanted to stop at Dave's to check on her car. Lila said they would set up their schedule over breakfast tomorrow. As she drifted off to sleep, she was thinking that just as she was getting Vinnie interested, Violet was thinking about going home.

Day 5: Monday

George insistently demanded, "Everybody up."

Lila woke up, wondering what day it was. *Oh yes, today we are going to check on Vi's car, go over to Goshen to heist a sewing machine, stop to see Mrs. Swanson, and if there was any time left, plant several rows of vegetables.* She thought that today was not going to be as enjoyable as yesterday. She quickly dressed and slipped down the stairs to put on coffee and brew tea. Benny helped her with letting out the free-range hens and checking on the bee barn. Out of habit, she made the garden inspection first, and then walked up to the bee barn. As she took a quick peek into the bee barn, she noticed that one of the afghan throws was missing from the hay bale couch. "Hmm, when did I take that back to the house? I have been going a little too hard and fast. I need to slow down after Violet leaves."

Violet was drinking tea and reading the paper when Lila walked in. "You know, Lila, I would really like to go with you when you go to see Marguerite's laboratory. It would be quite an adventure together, just like we used to do."

Surprised by her insistence and not sure that was a good idea, given her argument with Jed, Lila responded, "We will see, the timing depends on when Marguerite comes around to accepting my help." And then added, "I want to address something you said yesterday about the mockery which your mother endured. Please believe me, I always admired your mother for her spunk and freethinking. Your house was a happy one, full of life and verve. Sure, the ancestor seeings were staged, but all in good fun like a Shakespearean play, and she was an accurate forecaster."

"But," Violet countered, "everyone thought Daddy was crazy and that Mum was possessed."

"Not so," Lila said. "Not those of us who spent any time with your family. You had the best. Do you have any idea how many children in this world would have bargained their only pair of shoes for a chance to spend a summer at your house?"

On the way to Dave's, Violet was afraid that since they had not heard from him that he probably ran into some problems. Lila scolded, "Remember what you used to tell me when I would start fussing?"

Violet responded, "You're frying my nerves?"

Dave came out to the reception area with an apologetic look on his face, saying that he had good news and bad news. The good news is that the new parts came in but the bad news is that the new parts don't connect easily with the old parts, but he could find the needed connector piece over in Bailey's junkyard. In fact, he sent his man over there this morning. "Won't be able to get to your car before tomorrow morning as I am really jammed up today."

Violet, with her sweetest smile, said, "Please do because I do have to get home in a few days."

Back on the road to Goshen, they decided to stop at Mrs. Swanson's first as they did not want to interfere with her afternoon nap. With trepidation, they pulled into her driveway, gave each other a thumbs up, and went to the side porch door as was the custom. Lila knew that she had closed up all rooms, except several located in the back of the house: a maid's kitchen and a sleeping room. The maid was let go years ago. The grand front door had probably remained firmly locked ever since her husband died. Just as they were about to use the door knocker, Violet bumped Lila with a shush and put a cupped hand up to her ear. Piano music, just repetitive cords with a few mistakes thrown in. With quiet discussion, they knew that this was not the time to interrupt. They headed back to the car, but Lila noticed that Mrs. Swanson was now peeking out from the porch door, so they decided to be brave and approach again.

Well, yes, Mrs. Swanson said that she might be able to help with a few particulars about the Stanton homestead as her husband had kept very good records in his library. And as a matter of fact, a lady from the county historical society stopped the other day, wanting to know about the house. "Really," queried Lila, "Did she say why she was inquiring?"

Mrs. Swanson said, "I told her that I did not know any particulars and sent her packing. But she did make me curious enough to dust off a few ledgers, and I found some things which might be of interest to you." Lila was itching to see the library, and Violet was anxious to get a peek into the parlor. Finally she opened the door just wide enough for them to step into the kitchen. The kitchen was neat but very dated, as expected. She said, "You two wait here, have a seat at the table and I will bring the ledgers."

She slipped out into the hallway, closing the door firmly. Lila whispered, "We are making progress, one room at a time." Violet was starting to think that at this pace, she might not ever get into the parlor.

Mrs. Swanson brought out to the kitchen table three leather-bound notebooks that looked to have extensive information about the local area. All hand notations in pencil but quite legible. And sure enough, they found Violet's homestead, including the acreage, year built, and the first homesteader. Mrs. Swanson was warming up to the visit and added some personal anecdotes of what she remembered about arriving here with her new husband, just when the country was coming out of the depression. "I was a city girl and I thought this was absolutely the end of the world, but my husband had inherited sufficient funds to promise me we could travel and have a fine lifestyle. And we did for a while…" But then she trailed off and said, "Now you ladies are not interested in all this."

At this point, Violet said she was interested in where Mrs. Swanson received her musical training and she would be ever grateful if she would show them the parlor, and especially the piano. Mrs. Swanson said, "Not today as I have a cleaning lady coming. Why don't you come by tomorrow?"

Back in the car, Lila said, "You are amazing. I thought you jumped too far ahead, asking to see the piano, but you were right on target."

Violet chuckled and said, "Well, my time is running short, so we needed to light a candle."

Lila responded, "I'll bet she is in there, practicing the piano right now. Did you notice that she still has lovely long fingers?" Violet nodded and looked down at her own lovely piano hands. Lila giggled and said now that luck was on their side, they might pull off the sewing machine caper after all.

Traveling down the short lane to the Stanton homestead, they braked for twin fawns following their mother across their path. As they pulled up, Violet said they should hide the Jeep behind the barn until they managed to wrestle the Singer out to the patio door, then pull it closer. But Lila was afraid that if Vinnie did come by, he might not stop if he did not see her Jeep, so they decided to risk nosy neighbors and possibly Mr. Whitey Tightie cruising by.

Once inside, they both lingered at the overstuffed music equipment room door, wondering what all could be tossed in there. Hyacinth's Bello Cello was still on its side, over in the corner, and they talked about whether they should rescue it also. Lila allowed that there was not enough room in the Jeep after they managed to get the Singer into the back.

Lila said, "I still think we should search through that stuff for your music scores."

"Do you mean right now?"

"No, no, we don't have the time today, but eventually, before the place falls into other hands."

"I still think they went with the maple furniture."

"Well, then, I have another idea. We could post an ad in the local paper saying that we would like to purchase birds-eye maple bedroom furniture. That may be revealing and produce some results. Would you recognize the marks and blemishes on your pieces?"

"Yes, there were several scratches I could identify, unless it had been restored."

From there they moved into the music parlor, planning to hurry up with the move. Lila slowed things down by reminding Violet of the time that she walked in to find her grandma's foot pumping the Singer wheel at great speed, whipping up some new frock for one of the girls; by the color, she knew it was not a boy's shirt. Grandma told her to check in before she went home because she had something for her. She did check in, just as Grandma whipped out a beautiful dress. Yes, Violet did remember that dress because it was similar to one of hers and Grandma claimed that she got the idea because she did not have enough material for either Violet or Hyacinth, both much taller than Lila.

"Well, that may have been the case, but she had me try it on and it was still several inches too long, but she said I would grow into it. Well, I did, and I surely did march around in that dress, even Hildegarde was envious."

"No, not Hildegarde, she was only envious of her own dresses."

"Yes, Hildegarde, she asked me where I bought it and I told her at Shanebrooks."

"She shopped there all the time and probably knew it did not come from Shanebrooks."

"No, I told her it was the last one in stock and they would not be ordering more."

Just as they were laughing and lugging the machine out through the patio door, Vinnie came trundling up in his enclosed construction truck and volunteered to take the machine back to Lila's. They thought that was a great idea. After loading it, they both hid their vehicles behind the barn and went back into the house to give Vinnie an inside look. This took much longer than expected since he wanted to pick and push at all partitions, doors, and windowsills to check for rot and water damage. He even crawled up through a trapdoor to the attic. He was especially worried about the side of the house where the porch pulled away and he thought there was a little foundation damage on that side. And of course, there were many more things Violet remembered to tell him. But all in all, he was sure most problems could be remedied with money and time. Neither woman wanted to ask how much money and how much time. As they drove in tandem up to the road, who should come slowly cruising by but Mr. Deputy Sheriff man.

Vinnie called out, "Hi, Oscar, what brings you out this way?"

"Just doing my duty. What brings you out this way?"

"Just had a look around the outside. Town hall said okay since they own it now."

"I caught those two snooping around the other day, sent them packing"

"They were explaining some history to me. Violet was raised here."

Walking back to the Jeep and peering inside, sheriff man nodded a hello to both.

Lila nodded. Violet smiled. He slowly postured importantly back to his car. Violet chuckled, imagining him in his whities.

Lila glanced at Violet and said out loud, "Stop that."

They all drove away slowly and chuckling.

Back home, with the sewing machine safely tucked away at Lila's, they decided to take sandwiches and drinks out to the patio. Benny joined them for company. Violet was feeling pretty smug about securing Grandma's Singer and eluding Mr. Sheriff man. She said that she just might try out that old sewing machine just for old times' sake as Grandma had taught her a few tricks with buttons and bows. "Which reminds me," Lila asked, "whatever happened to that old wind up RCA Victrola you had in the music parlor? Remember Dinah Shore's rendition of 'Buttons and Bows?'" Violet jumped up and belted out several choruses:

> East is East and West is West
> And the wrong one I have chose
> Let's go where they keep on wearing
> Those frills and flowers
> and buttons and bows.

Laughing now and edging Violet on, Lila mentioned "Boogie Woogie Bugle Boy" by the Andrews Sisters. Of course, Violet hit her stride now, dancing and singing to "Boogie Woogie Bugle Boy" of Company B.

> A-toot, a-toot, diddleyada-toot
> He blows it eight to the bar, in boogie rhythm

With so much repeated use, they must have worn grooves in those old 78rpm records. Lila wondered if several might not have made it into the music equipment room under some of that stuff. She was pretty sure the old Victrola was not in there. Violet sat down, finished her drink, and said she was worn out now and wanted to take a nap. Lila thought that was a very good idea since she wanted to slip up to the garden and put in a couple rows of basil and beans, now that all threat of frost was long gone; even the oaks had leafed out two weeks ago. Wow, time was flying. She also wanted to make sure there was firewood and hotdog sticks up by the pit near the bee barn. It would be like old times, having a hotdog roast with Violet. Thinking ahead, she called Caroline, one of Violet's grade school chums.

Caroline was delighted to come for the hotdog roast. The wood was really dry, so the fire started easily after Lila found her matches. It was a firefly night with a promising half-moon on the rise, just over the house. Lila had extra sweatshirts in the bee barn for later. Caroline and Violet shared many amusing school stories. Caroline told them about the time that Violet's brother, Stanton Jr., threw Mrs. Williams' paddle out the school window. Well, it took her all of three minutes to figure who the paddle culprit was—the one that got the most paddling, of course. She pulled him by his ear all the way outside, made him pick up the paddle, hand it to her politely, to which we all applauded since we were standing at the window, watching. But then, she paddled him all the way back in. That was back in the day when teachers were allowed to handle their own discipline, of course.

Then Caroline revealed that she had purchased some furniture from the Stanton house when the Richards were moving; they lived there several years before moving to Seattle. Cautiously Lila asked which pieces she bought at the Richards' sale. Caroline said she got a fantastic price on some birds-eye maple bedroom furniture which she still owned. Violet, pushing forward to the edge of her seat, eagerly asked, "You didn't happen to notice some papers taped to the bottom of the second and third drawer?"

"Oh no," Caroline said, "I am sure not. I refinished the entire set, and I would have noticed anything like that. It turned out gorgeous by the way." Violet was happy that it was Caroline that got the Hy-Vi furniture but a little sad that her music scores were not found. And it made Lila a little more determined to have a look into that music room.

Lila did not want the lovely evening to end but the fire was dying down; Violet looked tired, and Caroline thought she had better be on her way. While Violet doused the fire, Lila ran into the bee barn to get the flashlight which she kept up there just in case of emergencies. But no flashlight to be found. Oh well, she must have laid it down somewhere else. Anyway there was enough moonlight to see them down to the house and Caroline's car.

In her nightclothes, Lila sat on the end of Violet's bed and asked her how she was feeling. Violet said in response that she could not thank Lila enough for all she had been doing to make her feel welcome and helping her with things, you know, such as the car. And that they had better check with Dave tomorrow afternoon to see if he got the new parts married to the old parts. Lila assured her that Dave was a mechanical surgeon and he should be operating at an orthopedic hospital somewhere.

Day 6: Tuesday

Over breakfast, they talked leisurely about Caroline and the coincidence of the furniture ending up with her. Violet said that it probably was not just a coincidence as she felt that there was a higher power directing events. Silently Lila thought that it would be too trifling for a higher power to be worried about furniture, but with a small nod to Violet, she kept that thought to herself. If higher power meddling gave Violet comfort so be it. Since the music was not sold with the furniture, Violet agreed that perhaps they might be able to sort through a little of the stuff in the music room, maybe even bring the Bello Cello back to Lila's place. She was not sure she could even get the Singer into her little car, let alone a washtub. But she was most excited to stop at Mrs. Swanson's today. "Do you think we might make it into the parlor today?"

"Violet, the first thing this morning, I have a scheduled session with Marguerite at the café."

"Perhaps I could tag along and meet Marguerite."

"No, not yet, but I will ask her if we could set up an appointment to go out to her cabin."

'Well then, I will just tag along today and flirt with Burt and Sonny."

"You always have all the fun."

"It runs in my family."

"No one could dispute that fact."

Pulling into the café, Lila noticed all the usual cars with the exception of Sonny's Chevy pickup. When they entered, Burt, with solemn importance, was telling everyone how it happened. Last night, traveling on the old Schoonover Road, Sonny swerved to miss several deer, just standing on the road. He lost control and went through the guardrail, into the ditch. You know it was right on Dead Man's Curve which is dangerous anytime of the year. This morning, he was still in Alma General Hospital with lacerations, bruises, and several broken bones. Rachel piped up and asked Burt whatever was he doing late at night, way over on the Schoonover Road. "Hell, Rachel, how would I know? I don't keep his schedule."

Someone else piped up and said that they knew that he had relatives from over that way. Lila hesitated before going back to the pantry, feeling the loss that everyone here would feel if Sonny's chair went empty. She also knew that the Schoonover Road led into the Hollow, the valley where Marguerite lived. That seemed to be a useful bit of information that she would mentally file under M. Lila gave the usual two dozen eggs to Jed, accepted two cups of coffee, and pushed back to the pantry.

Marguerite was all on task this morning with several cabbages already chopped for slaw and carrots scraped; she just sat down to peel potatoes when Lila entered. Lila noticed that Marguerite was looking a little more down than usual, but she did have on a clean sweatshirt that said, "Go Badgers," the local school mascot. That made Lila chuckle since Marguerite did look like a little badger this morning. As they settled into their routine of cooperation, Lila asked her what was in that milk poultice that she remembered her own mother using on her brother's boils. Marguerite thought that it was probably just that, milk and softened bread placed in a gauze sack, taped over the boil. Draws the boil to a head. Add tea tree essential oils, fights infection. Add fresh herbs, fights scale. Different ailments, different recipes. Lila smiled and said that she had a lot to learn. Marguerite glanced at her sideways.

"Marguerite," Lila bravely continued, "Jed tells me that you have been having equipment problems."

"Seems so."

"He thought that I might be able to help you with your equipment."

"I am thinking 'bout retiring."

"What about all those people over in the Hollow who depend on you?"

Silence.

"What about all those mothers with colicky babies and worse?"

Silence.

"Not to mention Jed's grandson."

Silence.

"What about your grandfather's legacy as a healer and physician? And his daddy and granddaddy! Marguerite, we cannot let all this knowledge just disappear, can we? Tomorrow morning, we are not scheduled here at Jed's, so I could come over to see what you need. I have access to lots of unused equipment at my old lab."

On the way over to Goshen to see Mrs. Swanson, before her nap time, Lila wanted to know if Violet heard any more gossip this morning. Violet said it got quiet after the accident news was hashed over and retold several times. Burt was setting up a schedule so as not to overburden Sonny with too many visitors at one time. Then Lila revealed to Violet that she convinced Marguerite to let her come over to her cabin tomorrow morning. Violet pumped her fist and exhaled. "Am I included in this adventure?"

"Yes, but remember, you are just a very good friend and bystander. You have to agree to just smile and keep your mouth shut."

"Well I am very good at that."

"Which, the smile part or the mouth-shut part?"

They both agreed that when and if they did get into the Swanson house that they were expecting damp dark musty cushion odors, perhaps combined with some mouse poops and fly droppings. After all, the main portion had been closed off and unheated for years. Great climate for mold, moths, and mildew. Lila added, "And cobwebs—don't forget the cobwebs."

Violet offered. "Just imagine how dangerous Mum could have been there," making both of them laugh, breaking the nervous tension.

As they were pulling into Mrs. Swanson's drive, Betsy was just pulling out. Betsy did odd jobs, even in Rockton where most people did the work themselves. Betsy was a jack of all trades, as they say. She could wallpaper, move stoves, and take care of someone just home from the hospital, perhaps all three at the same time. And she was affordable. "I wonder what she was doing here?"

"Well, I think we are about to find out!"

Just as the two started toward the side porch door, they heard Mrs. Swanson call, "No, no, over here, on the front porch." They both stopped short in their leaden feet. "Come in this way, please." Lila whispered through closed lips, "Did St. Anthony just arrive from Padua or am I imagining things?" Violet gave her a small nudge forward, she herself more excited than Lila.

Just stepping up onto the front porch made them feel privileged. Certainly a step-up from the days when Violet and Jimmy used to sneak around the back windows just for a peek. After Mrs. Swanson offered them porch chairs on which to sit, Violet was a little worried that this was as far as they would get today. But Lila was still hopeful. They had iced tea and a few crackers which did taste stale but only slightly; they were polite and ate them. Making idle conversation, they asked Mrs. Swanson about her background, where she was born, and where she got her education. Well, she was born in New York City, she said, but her daddy came from Ireland, looking for work, of course.

"He did find work all right and actually became quite successful as a construction manager at a very big firm, but he would have preferred to be a full-time musician. He was very good with the violin, but family responsibilities interfered with those plans. So instead, he sent both my sister and me to good music schools."

At the mention of music schools, Violet offered that she wished that she had gone on to study music. Hers was all by ear and guess.

As Mrs. Swanson grew quiet, Lila did not want to push her to allow them into the house. She was content to allow this porch visit to be the maximum step that they could take today, but Violet, running out of time and feeling a little desperate, knew it was now or never. Sucking up her courage and putting on her prize-winning smile, Violet said, "Mrs. Swanson, you would be doing me the greatest honor if you would allow me to just sit at your piano and imagine that I was playing at a great concert hall."

Mrs. Swanson came back with, "Yes, please do come in. I am afraid the place is not anything special and needs a great deal of work, but I did have the piano tuned. It is not perfect yet, but a few more tune-ups should bring it back into pitch. He was not happy about it being kept in the unheated parlor, but the cost of heating this grand lady is exorbitant."

With a slight gimp in her step, Mrs. Swanson worked her way to the door, twisted the brass handle, and gave the door a little shove. She stood back and allowed an amused smile creep into the corners of her mouth. "Well, go on, you two."

Somehow it did not feel right to go in ahead of her, so they hesitated but looked at each other and stepped inside, and just stood there, speechless; even Violet who was traveled enough now that this simple country home should not have impressed her. After all, she had toured the Biltmore several times. But this Goshen country home was exactly what did impress her. The breezes from the open windows were rustling the drapes and a ray of sunshine was playing fickle with the crystals in the chandelier. Lila could not resist running her hand along the magnificent stairwell, and Violet was soaking in the lush five-inch molding snugging up to the ceiling.

Lila sent Violet a secret message across invisible ether waves—*"Betsy"*. Violet smiled. All doors leading into the foyer and hallway had been thrown open. From where she stood, Lila could peek into the library and Violet was straining to look in the other direction. She knew from her childhood forays that the grand piano was back in the music parlor. Both waited for Mrs. Swanson to take the lead.

Mrs. Swanson proudly led them into the front sitting parlor. It did indeed have exquisite wallpaper, even though now somewhat tinged with age. The upholstery on the divan and chairs had mellowed into pleasant shades of burnt umber and magenta, featuring peacocks and peach trees with angelic maidens in attendance. There was an early nineteenth-century tapestry with silken thread on the interior wall that depicted a parlor scene with a stunning woman playing a grand piano. Admiringly, a little family was cozily gathered around her with their punch cups in hand. Violet gave a little sigh as she studied it. In contrast to this exquisite decorating, a very stern portrait, hung above the fireplace, glared sternly down at them; and a lady's portrait, on the opposite wall, haughtily stared over at her husband's portrait. There seemed to be many messages flying about the room.

When Mrs. Swanson saw Lila studying her father-in-law's portrait, she said, "After my husband died, I started to take that painting down but decided I liked it there. I can come in and tell him what a grinch he had been. He did not take good care of his employees, overworked and underpaid them. And then his wife, Genevieve over there, never approved of me. She thought she was Nefertiti, queen of the Nile. After I discovered that she was originally from the Hollow, I called her Nefertiti of Swamp Hollow, only behind her back of course. Now I say it to her face." Both Lila and Violet chuckled. "Don't get me wrong, ladies, my husband was a different sort, kind and affectionate. He adored me—we had a good life here, even though I could not fill the house with little ones." Lila offered that perhaps it was not her fault. "My dear." She sighed. "They always blame the wife."

Finally the temptation was just too great, and Violet, on her own volition, wandered into the music parlor. She made a complete circle around the piano as though she had to reign in her emotions, and perhaps, encourage the piano to submit to her will. As an adult, Violet has had many opportunities to play grand pianos; her son even wanted to purchase one for her. But it was this piano which held her dreams and her heart. It was only a stone's throw away from her childhood home, but it was as unreachable as Venus or Mars. Violet sat down and began to play, slowly and tentatively at first, but she quickly gained confidence when she realized that this instrument would be a willing partner to her musical skills. Lila and Mrs. Swanson remained in rapt attention. Lila, of course, did not know what she was playing, only that it was hauntingly beautiful. Adrift in the moment, Mrs. Swanson sat down and closed her eyes. Watching these two pianists, Lila was reminded of all the lost chances in life. Two concert pianists who could have known and loved each other, played together, taught each other, but for slipping through the cracks of timing, except for this one too late *now*.

As Lila turned the Jeep down the lane to the old homestead, Violet said that she was a little tired and not in the mood to sort through the music room today. "But, Violet, we are running out of time. We really need to see if your music scores are in there and whatever else."

"Well, anyway, I might have to stay an extra day if Dave has not fixed my car yet."

"I would be happy for you to stay, you know that."

Violet suggested that she did want to wander up to see if they could find Baby Rose's stone. Lila had forgotten about the little family burial plot which used to be carefully maintained by Holly with a carefully planted flower garden, not to mention the most beautiful rose, twining around an archway. The markers, probably rotted away by now, had been handwritten on wood as no one could afford granite, but each grave had been carefully outlined with stones.

As they kicked at the bramble of vines and grasses, which had all but taken over, they did locate the approximate area which should have been Baby Rose's grave. They also found a piece of wood that was now too worn to read but that was probably her marker. Lila suggested that they get a nice piece of wood from Vinnie and etch Rose's name on it with her woodburning tools and bring it back tomorrow. Perhaps bring some clippers to clear the area a bit. This seemed to bring Violet back in spirits. As they headed back to the car, Lila mentioned that they had not yet had the time to tour the barn. But Violet wanted to stop to check on her car, so she was anxious to go back to Rockton and skip the barn tour today.

Dave's receptionist was hand-holding several unhappy customers when they walked in. She signaled for them to take a seat. Finally with problems resolved, she told them that Dave was out on a call and he wanted to talk with Violet before she took the car. It was fixed, she thought, but could they stop back tomorrow? Violet wanted to know if he had written up her bill yet. No, they would have that ready for her tomorrow. Lila wished she would stop worrying about the bill as she planned to pay for it as a present for Violet.

Vinnie was hurrying past just as they arrived home, so Lila flagged him down to ask for a piece of preserved wood to use as a grave marker. "You want the darnedest things, Lila. Whatever will you want next?"

"Oh, you can be sure I will come up with something weird."

He said he would stop down after washing up. Lila gave Violet a glass of cucumber-infused water and coaxed her to put her feet up for a few minutes. She would take Benny up to the hen yard and check the garden.

Lila carried water to the henhouse and checked their boxes. All seemed normal; with Bridgette playing boss, the hens were settled into the new pecking order. The garden was getting dry, so Lila was hoping for that promised rain tomorrow, "I will have to start watering. Vinnie was right, I should install an irrigation pipe down from the run. Lugging the hose up from the house is getting old. I will investigate that after violet leaves. Okay, Benny, a quick inspection of the bee barn and then back to fix a quick supper."

At the bee barn, the door was ajar so they went inside, but all looked normal; but Lila was wondering why the door was slightly ajar. She thought she closed it firmly last night after the roast, but maybe she was distracted about not having a flashlight to guide Caroline to her car.

It was a nice evening for supper on the patio. Violet was fixing the salad when Lila walked in. She looked up and asked if the hens were in for the night. "Yes," Lila responded, "All is well. I will just throw the casserole in the oven, and then we will sit outside with a glass of wine."

With a tiny shake of the head, Violet said, "Only a tiny glass for me, please. I am not supposed to have more than a thimbleful."

Lila was thinking about that comment when Caroline drove up and said she wanted to say goodbye in case Violet was leaving tomorrow. But Lila explained that Violet was not leaving for several more days because she does not have her car yet and they had a big day planned for tomorrow. Caroline said she would join them for a glass of wine, but she already had her supper.

As the storytelling began, everyone knew to sit back and let Caroline hold sway. Her shoulders would tremble before her laugh emerged into full melody, then you knew a story was coming. She said Violet's brother, little Jimmy, used to come over to play with her little brother.

"One summer, they decided to build a lookout fort which started with bits and pieces of wood from their basement. As it grew, they begged or borrowed lumber and nails from who knows where. This fort was becoming quite the hangout for the neighborhood boys. Finally they decided to put on a second story with a circular staircase. They painted it with an odd assortment of colors and wrote 'lookout-fort' in red letters above the door. The second story had two windows, one for watching for Indians coming up the driveway and one which looked out toward the neighbor's house next-door. Well, as it happens, the cutest little young lady lived next door and her bedroom window was exactly opposite the fort window. As she was getting dressed one day, she walked over to the window just as one of the boys, we never knew which one, was peering out the fort window. Well, she went screeching to her mother and her mother came screeching to my mother, insisting we tear down that horrible thing. When Dad came home, he straightened things out, made them board up that offending window, but with a wink, he told the boys that they should have called it a look-in fort."

True to his word, Vinnie drove up with the board for Baby Rose's grave marker, and he agreed to stay for wine; but he did not want to stay for supper, said he had plans. Lila was thinking, maybe he just did not like the looks of the vegetarian casserole. She could not blame him as she was also thinking it looked a little bland. She knew she should have practiced with those vegetarian casseroles before Violet came. Vinnie said he had been doing a little more investigating about the old homestead and various town board members figured that it could be bought very reasonably and they would try again to get in touch with Mr. Williams. With that info, Caroline's eyes lit up, showing interest.

Caroline said that she needed more room for her horses, and as she remembered, there was quite a bit of property there. Violet volunteered that unless someone sold off parcels that there should be fifty-seven acres. Lila shot Violet a *"hush"* signal over the airwaves, changed the subject, and asked Vinnie what kind of conduit she should buy for her irrigation pipe. Well, Caroline piped up with all the answers as she had just run a line down from Alder Run for her horse trough. She figured she was done with running a hose over from the springhouse. Quickly she offered to help Lila when she wanted to get started as long as it was not on one of her teaching days; her riding academy was growing bigger every day.

Lila said, "I understand you are working wonders with the handicapped children."

"Well, that is nice to hear," Caroline responded, "but I need a spotter. I am looking for a young lady who could spend a few hours a week in turn for free riding time."

"If I hear of anyone, I will call," Lila said.

Violet piped up, "Just go down to Jed's in the morning. They know everybody's business down there."

MOSTLY ON SUNDAY

Vinnie offered his goodbyes and wished Violet luck with her car. As Caroline was saying her goodbyes and wishing Violet could come more often, she said she remembered something she wanted to tell her. We just got too busy with other stories around the hotdog fire.

"When the Richards had their three-day sale at your old homestead, they had awfully high prices on everything the first two days. I bought the bedroom outfit on the first day because I knew it would go quickly, especially being birds-eye maple, and I've never regretted one penny. However, I was also hankering for the RCA Victrola, my goodness, you would never guess how much they wanted for it. Well, when I went back on Sunday, they had it marked down from ninety-five dollars to sixty-five dollars. I figured it was too great to pass up, and I knew you would be happy that it went to a good home. 'Heavy as sin' because the records were in the cabinet below."

After that revelation, Caroline said that this was probably goodbye for now, hugged Violet, and said she could find her way to the car. Lila gave Violet a *"Well, now, what else might she have?"*

By now, Lila realized that it was getting too late to push Violet to talk about her scheduled doctor's appointment, but she did ask her if she thought there might be a chance she would move back here someday. Violet thought that perhaps she had lived in the South for so long now that she was more like a summer zinnia rather than a tough lilac. Laughing, Lila countered and said she just hoped that her best friend was not becoming a shrinking violet, making them both chuckle. Violet offered that maybe it would be a good thing to have Caroline buy the farm, knowing she would be great on the upkeep, and that way, she could always come back for a visit and not have all the worries.

Lila offered, "And I suppose she would bring back the birds-eye and the Victrola."

After rehashing the events of the evening, Violet headed for the shower and Lila went to her craft room to burn the name "Baby Rose" and a rose symbol into the new grave marker. Perhaps she could get some dates and burn that in later.

Day 7: Wednesday

Shortly after George made his wake-up call, Lila jumped out of bed to get the chores done early as they had a big day ahead. Last night, before going to sleep, she realized that she was getting anxious about this trip to Marguerite's, what with finding the place, taking Violet with her, and wondering if Marguerite would accept help or suggestions. From her alchemist readings, she realized that with modern laboratory equipment, she could probably improve on her procedures; but she might have to teach her about polarity, molecular weights, electron transfer, substrates, and membrane porosity. In her mind, it was beginning to amount to a college major in biochemistry.

With coffee and tea brewing, she and Benny raced up to let the hens out. Bridgette led the way with George looking on, proud as a peacock. Just then, a helicopter came circling overhead, quite low. *Odd*, thought Lila. The little airport over in Alma had only small private planes and only occasionally she would see someone flying over, but never a helicopter. Perhaps her neighbors could speculate on this activity. Jack had a two-way radio antenna right outside of his house, and he kept up with police and fire reports. Jack and Jewel kept a close eye on all neighborhood traffic, and she knew they kept an observant eye on her house, right from their kitchen window, giving Lila much comfort. Returning to her chores, she made a quick inspection of the garden and the bee barn, but all was normal. Over a quick breakfast, they made plans for the day. Both agreed that it would be best to stop at Dave's first before he got called out somewhere. Violet was anxious about why he wanted to see her if the car was already fixed.

Dave's receptionist, armed with her brand-new communication system with a speaker hanging down her chest and earbuds in her ears, announced, "Dave, please come to the front. You have two customers."

Lila was now wondering if perhaps they were paying Dave too much. Smiling confidently and carefully wiping his hands in a towel, Dave came out, greeting them, and said that he thought the car was fixed. He took it out for a short spin yesterday and it was performing okay. But he wanted Violet to run the car a couple of days before she started out on a long journey, especially by herself. Privately Violet was a little offended by that remark but let it pass. She had been taking long journeys by herself for a long time now and was doing just fine. Dave also suggested that she might want to think about trading it in when she got back home for a newer, more reliable model. Lila was thinking, *Not before it made it into Ripley's*. The bill was reasonable, and Violet whipped out her checkbook before Lila had a chance to intercede.

Violet offered to drive her car over to Marguerite's, but Lila declined. Both understood why. "We will take your car this afternoon when we go over to your homestead."

They hung Marguerite's directions up on the visor and headed out. Lila knew how to get to Schoonover Road, but the other two roads were unfamiliar. After seven miles on Schoonover, they slowed down at Dead Man's Curve where they noticed black tire marks, upturned soil divots, and a gouge in the ditch. Both ladies groaned a little (eight more miles, watch for Hardscabble Road off to the right, take that right, after nine miles, you will come to a T with a stop sign, turn left, staying on Hardscrabble two more miles, you will come to a little dirt road called Possum Crossing. The sign is tiny but legible. There are two mailboxes at the entry. Drive up that road several miles. You will pass a large house on the left with many old cars sitting around. An automechanic lives there, a good one too, keeps my old car running).

Well it turned out easier than either expected. They came up Possum Crossing, through the woods, out to a small clearing, and Marguerite's cabin came into view. They sat there for a minute, expecting a large dog to greet them. Nothing, except a muffled throaty bark and the sound of their own blood thrumming through their ears. Sitting in the car, taking in the surroundings for a moment, they realized that the cabin was rustic and country charming. The added-on laboratory in the back was rather makeshift but sound-looking. There were several garden plots in the front and more on the side with very healthy patches of herbs and plants. One plot on the side had some eight-foot-tall plants which Lila did not recognize. But then, she probably would not recognize any of the others either.

Finally Marguerite's little head peeked out of the laboratory door, so they took that as their welcome. Both got out of the car slowly, and with Lila in the lead, they approached the half-opened door cautiously. With Marguerite still undecided, half-in half-out, Lila smiled and said she hoped that Marguerite didn't mind terribly that she brought a friend as she did not want to come out by herself. Marguerite blinked twice, but Lila did not understand that code so she forged on and asked her if she would mind showing them her wonderful gardens. Marguerite, still silent, stepped out and led the way to the front patch which held common herbs that everybody grows. She definitely was not ready to tour them around to the back private gardens.

After this little tour, Marguerite paused at the door, sizing up Violet. Violet had been warned to keep her mouth tightly closed, but Violet never listened to Lila—why should she start now? "Marguerite, I am Cliff Stanton's daughter, perhaps you might have heard of him."

A slow realization came over Marguerite's face as she said, "Holly's daughter." In stunned silence, they all stood there, waiting for the next moment to pass. Marguerite broke the silence and said, "Sorry about Baby Rose. I did all I could." Now with time pregnantly pausing, the three stood there quietly, digesting that information. Nervous, Lila was trying to sift some soil below her shoe. This time, Violet broke the silence, she smiled!

Marguerite turned to the door and stepped in lightly with both women cautiously following. All three stopped after their first step inside, allowing their eyes to adjust to the calming and reduced lighting inside. Completely overwhelmed with the complexity of the laboratory, Lila felt her heart do a somersault as it sometimes does when too excited. Words to describe the essence of the scene displayed here were beyond the reach of Lila's vocabulary. Perhaps Charles Dickens could have done it descriptive justice, but regrettably, she was poorly schooled in the fine arts. She knew her silence was sending Marguerite a message which she could not fail to grasp. Feet firmly planted, she allowed her eyes to glide around the room. The sink, water bath, incubator, and a small oven were on a tall bench, just inside the door within reach. The glassware and experimental implements were neatly placed on or under a large table in the middle of the room. Everything was clean and functionally organized. A two-foot-tall glass tube, full of some essence, was dripping into a grass-like mesh disk, several inches thick, and then dripping into a flask, drip, drip, drip. Lila had the feeling that it was keeping time with some ancient practice.

Above the middle bench, ribbon-tied herbs were hanging from the rafters, drying, imparting a garden essence. Two walls were lined with shelves, each one carefully labeled: tonics, tinctures, elixirs, salves, essences, salts, spirits, oils, toxins, herbs, spices, grains, seeds, dried fruit, and pits. Each shelf held numerous individually labeled green mason jars with glass lids secured with a rubber ring and the wire band forcing tight closure. These jars were catching and reflecting several streams of light coming in from several small high-level windows and seemed to be carrying on a conversation among themselves. Who knows but what Marguerite could hear what they had to say?

There were storage cabinets underneath the shelves. In the next corner, there was a gigantic woodburning stove, for heat no doubt, and the biggest dog bed imaginable was in front of it. Several ancient side by side desks lined the interior wall, and the wall above was decorated with some ancient Chinese and Egyptian poster-size manuscripts. Beside the right-hand desk, there was a door leading into the cabin. There were some throaty questioning snuffs coming through that door. He was certainly ready to be called into service should he be needed.

Right here, in this unlikely spot, was generation upon generation of industry and knowledge. Violet, for once, was speechless, and Lila was as close to the *now* as she was ever going to be. Gravity was pulling her feet to the floor. This was ancient Spagyric Egyptian knowledge, probably influenced by the Indian Ayurveda medical practices first before passing through France, wending its way to the Appalachians. As Lila was coming back to her senses, she captured an instant insight. Marguerite does not need isoelectric gels for electrophoresis; she does not need substrates to separate molecular weights. She does not need speed. She only needs help replacing worn-out equipment.

The silence was palpable, and Lila, breaking the spell, spoke in almost a whisper, "Marguerite, we are honored to be here. We have only a slight knowledge of your art and please know that we will keep our silence about your lab if you wish it so."

Violet acknowledged that statement with a nod. Lila knew that Marguerite always measured her words, so she was not expecting a response and she did not get one. She simply nodded, and it did not seem to be a yes or no. In order to break through this barrier and start out with simple requests, Lila said, "We would be interested in hearing about your herbs and perhaps how one or two might be processed and utilized in your practice."

Marguerite was still silent, no doubt deciding how much to share, and perhaps it did not help that an additional person came along today. Reading Lila's thoughts, Violet asked if she could step outside and perhaps walk through some of the herb beds. Marguerite nodded affirmatively, so Violet slipped quietly out the door.

Now with this more comfortable setting, Marguerite did open up and led Lila over to the collected herb samples, some very common and others that she had never heard of before.

Lila said, "I did want to ask you about the horsetail plant. I remember my grandmother putting horsetail salve on skin rashes. I understand that it is an ancient plant from the carboniferous period, 350 million years ago. Does horsetail grow around here?"

"Yes, there are several species in our marsh areas, but one must be careful because some species can be toxic if administered internally in large doses. Your grandmother was probably using *Equisetum arvense* which can be safely used for rheumatism and gout or externally for rashes. Do you have any of her recipes?"

"No, they are either lost, thrown out, or possibly passed down to Bonnie, my cousin. But I have her *1919 Encyclopedia of Medicinal Preparations* which is still readable. I will look in there because that was, more than likely, her source."

"Yes, in the old days, very few people had access to a local doctor, so the women became very skilled in in-home treatment. But all of us need to remember that with all medicines, natural or synthetic, the poison is not only in the dose but also in drug interactions."

Then Lila noticed a jar that had been labeled with three components: turmeric, ginger, and Boswellia; she had never heard of

Boswellia. Marguerite said it was a resin from a tree in India but easy to purchase by mail order. However, she reprocessed it to make sure it was pure as some of the products one orders are laced with other ingredients. Marguerite did not offer how it might be used, so Lila guessed stomach disorders.

Marguerite said, "Arthritis, joint pain. If you don't have purified Boswellia, I recommend making a tea with turmeric, ginger, and cinnamon, sweetened with raw honey. Lila's, of course."

Lila then questioned, "What do you have for stomach disorders?"

"Depends. Is it for stomach or intestines? There are many combinations that worked for stomach and intestinal disorders. Depends on the problem."

"Well, let's focus on intestinal."

Marguerite pointed out seven or eight jars of grains, herbs, and spices that she uses in those preparations. Lila noticed a combination labeled Chinese which contained bok choy, garlic, ginger, and peppers. Marguerite assured her it was good for the intestines as well as the blood. Lila told her that since she liked bok choy, that she might like that one. Mar smiled and said that it helped people lose weight too, "But you do not need that…yet."

Lila smiled and was thinking that she would add garlic, ginger, and peppers to her braised bok choy and soy sauce preparations. She was also wondered out loud if Marguerite was a good cook. Mar answered, "No need anymore."

When they came to the elixirs, Lila could see that they mostly contained three or four ingredients maximum. In her book, Lila had read about an elixir that contained fourteen ingredients and claimed that it "helped" with many and varied health problems.

Marguerite frowned and said, "One should be cautious about putting too many different essences into one elixir. It is better to focus on one or perhaps two problems, if they are related, but too many ingredients at once may just confuse the natural healing process. Create mass confusion for the organic systems, so to speak."

"I notice that you have quite a stock of turmeric, ginger, cinnamon, and garlic powder."

"Yes, and don't forget the nutmeg."

Lila said, "The Nutmeg Wars played a vital role in shaping world empires, I understand."

"Great Britain won that battle, I believe, planted their own trees," Mar replied.

Wow, Lila thought, *She might have been home schooled, but she knows her history.*

Also there seemed to be several elixirs containing black cohosh which Lila knew was a native plant in the buttercup family. She remembered that her mother and grandmother took a preparation made from the root of the cohosh plant and they said it was for female problems which Lila took to mean menstrual and menopause problems. Marguerite said that she was careful not to give it to young females since pregnant women should not take cohosh.

This conversation opened the door to a subject dear to Lila's interest: the underrepresentation of women in the testing trials of new drugs. Having access to the literature, she knew that many trials included only male subjects. Marguerite said that in her experience, men and women often reacted differently to her tonics and elixirs. Lila suggested that the monthly cycle probably affected all sorts of problems with drug-standardized testing. The variability of hormonal fluctuations would create some of the problems, and it is well-known that women absorb drugs at a vastly different rate from men, at least until menopause.

Lila wanted to broach the subject of Jed's grandson's illness, but she wanted to ease into it because she knew Marguerite would guard her prescriptions as proprietorial information. Lila did not want to spy or play detective. She was only here to help because Jed asked her to come. But on the other hand, if she did open up, perhaps we all had something to learn from her alchemy.

"Marguerite, I understand that you helped Jed's grandson with some problems."

Marguerite replied, "Uh-huh."

"Jed said that you could not supply him with more medicine… broken equipment?"

Marguerite replied, "Uh-huh. Alembic broken."

"Marguerite, I would like very much to see your equipment. But perhaps, first we should go out to find Violet."

In a beautiful butterfly garden, behind the cabin, they found Violet closely inspecting a milkweed plant, looking at a butterfly chrysalis. The garden was alive with many winged inhabitants of various shapes and sizes. Naturally Lila looked for honeybees. Violet complimented Marguerite on this outstanding garden and asked her if she maintained all these beds by herself. Mar explained that she did have little Brittany who helps weed one day a week and Sonny comes to help now and then or when he can. *"Sonny!"*

"Of course, he won't be coming for a while. Had an accident, you know."

Silence! "He is my cousin on Uncle Sidney's side." Silence!

They moved over to a large stone and sat down in the shade of a ginkgo tree. Violet asked her about the dog who was now insisting to be let out. "Most people are very frightened of him, and that is okay with me, living up here alone as I do. If you ladies wait right here, I will take him out for just a moment."

Having heard about the dog from Jed, they decided to be very quiet and wait in the butterfly garden. This gave Lila a chance to explain to Violet some of what she saw inside. Violet said that she did not mind spending more time if Marguerite would allow her to go inside while they went over the equipment. "And I promise to be very quiet." However, Lila was a little suspicious about that comment. Violet added, "No, really, I promise."

When Marguerite came back to the butterfly garden, she addressed Violet directly and said that she regretted that she was not able to help Baby Rose. "When I saw the baby that night, I knew immediately that it was diphtheria and your mother confirmed that Rose had not received the DPT vaccine. I recommended that they get in touch with Doc Patterson right away for the antitoxin as it was far too late for antibiotics. It is the toxin which causes the strangulation and not the microorganism. Since I am not a licensed physician, I cannot get access to the antitoxin. And inasmuch as diphtheria can spread through air contact, I advised her not to allow any of you children into the room. That was the best I could do for her. I am so sorry." Violet reached out and gave a soothing touch on Marguerite's shoulder.

From the garden, the three moved back into the laboratory to discuss the equipment that was worrying Marguerite. Lila stepped toward the ancient water-bath incubator which, according to Marguerite, was still functioning, but Lila saw that the controls were outdated with only a hi and lo setting. Lila had contacts over at the Brookfield Plant where she still acted as a consultant. She knew she could obtain a water bath with settings that escalated with a sliding centigrade scale, allowing accurate control of temperature. Also she noticed the lack of an emulsifier and a tabletop centrifuge. Understanding the time it took for hand mixing and gravity sedimentation, she understood now why her preparations required a biblical month.

However, there was probably beauty and grace in waiting and watching the process develop over time, a reverence. One did not have that leisure time back at Brookfield Chemical. Next Marguerite's incubator was there but unplugged with a bare cord hanging down over the counter. Obviously Mar had been trying to fix it. That may still be possible, but Lila said she could get a newer model from spares at the chemical plant. With all this experimental technical language, Violet wandered over to look at the various jars of preparations. Marguerite did not take much notice, perhaps that absolving touch in the garden put Marguerite at ease.

Finally they came to the broken alembic, a handed-down piece of ceramic art, something that Lila had only just read about in *The Art of Alchemy*. It had been part of Marguerite's heritage and had probably been brought over to the new country on some ship arriving at the port in Philadelphia, many years ago. An alembic is a small tower with a tiny fireplace in the bottom where different sources of heat could be used, depending on the heat required. Further up on the walls, there were various portals, allowing for air control. The top contained a hollowed-out basin for a water bath into which one could place a flask of liquid contents. By heating the contents of this flask, one could vaporize the contents and then condense the vapor back into a liquid (distillation) down through connected cooling flasks which were in series. Each step down in the series cooled the material further. The further down the series, one collected different materials with different properties.

After investigation, Lila told Marguerite that she did not believe that the crumbling alembic could be repaired for safe use, but it could be restored as a family heirloom. There is a ceramist in Alma who would take on the alembic restoration as a fun project and she was very reasonable. Lila offered that it could be easily replaced with modern equipment that should not take Marguerite long to master. Watching a frown grow on Marguerite's face, she assured her that all of the equipment was used and would cause very little expense, if at all. She needed to make a trip over to Brookfield anyway.

They joined Violet who was sitting at one of the antique desks, admiring the spines of very old leather journals containing labels dating back to 1891. There was a plaque on the wall above the desk that read, "Through Nature, I am an Instrument of God." This place was not only a medical laboratory but also a shrine. As they were saying their goodbyes, Lila told Marguerite that she may not see her at Jed's tomorrow because she had some things to do before Violet left. But she still wanted to discuss her face-hydrating cream sometime in the future. "You would probably have some helpful hints, and we could produce it as a joint project."

On the way back through Rockton, they stopped to pick up Violet's car and agreed that they still had time to stop at Jed's for a sandwich. It was only 1:15 p.m. and Jed was open until 2:00 p.m. They ordered a quick sandwich and reported to Jed that they made their trip out to the Hasting Hollows. Jed whistled an approval and asked how it went. Violet said much better than she expected. Lila said that in a quieter moment, she would give him a full report but did he know that Sonny was related to Marguerite? "Yes, I thought so since he was the one who put me in touch with her in the first place."

They agreed that Violet needed to test-drive her car, but they decided to take both cars out to Goshen, just in case her car had some further problems. Dave seemed to be a little concerned about the rebuilt carburetor. Lila had loaded Baby Rose's grave marker and some gardening tools into the Jeep earlier this morning. Violet was getting eager to search around in the old family plot to look for relics to see if she could identify the grave location of her great-great-grandparents, Niles and Nyla.

Lila was thinking, *Uh-oh, I will have to make another marker.* After cutting away the vines and brambles, some stones became visible and they thought that they could identify at least seven graves. Violet was sure that the two main central graves were Niles and Nyla, so they decided to mark it thus. Lila could bring over a maker later. The one closest to the house, she thought was Baby Rose, so they took extra care to reset the stones and pound in the grave marker. Violet sat right down on the ground to visit with Baby Rose, and Lila gave her grieving space. The sun was sinking and the ladies were running out of energy, so it was decided that it was too late to tackle the music room. They would go on home, call it a day, and figure out Violet's departure schedule. But when Violet tried to start her car, it gave a sputtering sound. The battery was strong, so it probably was carburetor trouble. On the way back home, they stopped at Dave's, but it was locked up tight.

Just as they were putting together a little supper, Vinnie stopped in to say goodbye to Violet since he thought she would be leaving in the morning. He had not had supper yet, so Lila invited him to stay and have a glass of wine and stay for supper. Just as the three sat down for wine, Lila had to run in for another glass—Caroline stopped by. Lila was relishing all this company, even if Violet was the attraction. How she hoped that Violet would consider moving back to Goshen. With dinner over, dishes washed, friends departed, they sat out in the cool evening under the stars and planned tomorrow. First they would contact Dave about Violet's car, and it looked like her departure would be delayed for at least one day.

"Violet, it is past time that you confide in me about your medical appointments."

"Well, it's a long story."

"Take all the time you need."

"I have breast cancer."

Silence!

"I have already had a round of radiation and chemotherapy. It came back…My doctor wants to schedule another round soon.

Lila, I know what you are thinking, *"second opinion"*…I have had a second opinion over at Duke Medical. It is a vicious form. That is why I wanted to come back for a few days, just in case the worst happens…I am sorry that I did not call you. You are not shocked, I can tell."

"Violet, I think you should call your doctor and your son tomorrow and warn them that you have been delayed. If Dave finds your car unsafe, I will drive you back home this weekend. We really must go over and sort through that music room tomorrow. I would really like to find the music scores for your son."

Day 8: Thursday

George did not care that the ladies stayed up late and wanted to sleep in just a little. It took Lila a moment to realize why she felt a little down this morning, more than usual, that is. She tiptoed around, trying not to wake Violet, started coffee and tea, and with Benny, headed for the henhouse. She hoped that Violet would not hear George crowing since her bedroom was on the other side of the house. As usual, Benny was also anxious to go through their morning routine and the hens were anxious to start their day, and life goes on. If George doesn't wake her, that helicopter surely will. *Second day in a row and so low? This is strange. I still have not had the time to check in with Jack and Jewel to see what they know. Also we should stop down at Jed's because someone there will know something about this helicopter surveillance. Burt keeps his eyes in the air and his nose to the ground.*

Over coffee and toast, lavishly spread with peanut butter and honey, Lila brought out two more grave markers, one for Niles and one for Nyla. "Oh, Lila, you are special. I heard you coming to bed late."

Lila said that they would stop by her mailbox and Violet could pick out three stones from the pile there, pretty ones that she rescued when tilling the garden. Then they would stop by Dave's garage and see if he could rescue Violet's car which they had abandoned over in Goshen yesterday. Just as they were pulling out, Roger, in his white prison truck, was slowing and pulled to the side. Lila stopped and rolled down her window. Coming so early, he obviously had a message. He said that he was looking for a senior citizen, male, sixty-five years of age. His family over in Bloomsburg reported him missing several weeks ago. Apparently he started out for a doctor's appointment but he never made it. Some kids found his car abandoned in a field at the bottom of the lookout trail, but he was not in it.

"Did they try a bloodhound to trail him?" Lila asked.

"The Alma K9 unit tried, but with so many streams over there, they lost the trail."

"Maybe I should offer Benny, he is always sniffing something out."

"Well, I just wanted to warn you, ladies, and check on your car troubles."

"Lila's mechanic seems to have everything under control," Violet responded.

Looking over past Lila, Roger winked. "The offer is still good if you change your mind."

"Thanks, and thanks again for helping me out. I will be heading home soon."

They stopped at Dave's and were lucky to catch him, just as he was arriving at work. Dave was a little surprised to see them, but he was his usual calm self. They explained that the car was over in Goshen at the old Stanton house and they could not get it started yesterday. Dave said that he would follow them over there and see what he could do.

After a few failed attempts, Dave got his toolbox out and did a little adjusting with Violet behind the wheel. Grind, grind, grind. Adjust, adjust, adjust. *RRRRRRRrrrrromm.*

"Okay, keep it running for a few minutes. Shut it down and start it up again. Success! Keep it running. Shut it down and start again. Success! It was just the timing. It was not set properly. You'll be all right now."

"Thanks Dave, we will stop by to pay you."

"On the house, ladies. Drive safe!"

Lila knew she owed Dave another coffee cake, and he knew it too as he flashed her a conspiratorial look.

Both ladies wanted to head straight to the family burial plot. It took four trips from the car to the gravesite to lug stones, grave makers, hammers, and tools up there. They still had some gardening work they wanted to do. They cleaned around seven graves, and Violet felt pretty certain about the location of Niles's, Nyla's, and Baby Rose's grave. Violet selected and placed the stones for each of the three graves, and then Lila held the name markers while Violet wielded the hammer. They observed a moment of silence.

As Violet was hauling stuff out of the music room, Lila was categorizing the piles with a name attached, if possible. The biggest pile was for Cliff and Holly Stanton, but the Stanton children had lots of memories stuffed in there as well, plus there was a pile that Lila just marked "trash." She brought some black bags. Also there was a pile marked "unknown;" they would just pitch that stuff back into the room for the next owner to sort. Caroline would have a good time with that. Violet found a couple of boxes so she could haul a few things home for her son and for brother Jimmy. She was anxious to take her father's handcrafted mandolin as a present for her son. She had hoped to find some of his tuning tools, but he must have taken all those when he moved. Holly had saved all her correspondence and cards that she received over the years, and Violet thought they would make for interesting reading, so she decided to take all of it and sort through it at home.

Lila yelled, "Hey, Violet, have you found the commode yet?"

Violet stuck her head out and said, "No, but I found something amazing."

"What, your music scores?"

"No, something even more amazing."

"Not possible."

"Did you know that my mother was certified to teach primary school?"

"No, I didn't, but I am not surprised."

"Why didn't she ever teach?"

"Because some handsome fellow came along and asked her to hitch her wagon to his dreams."

Violet finally worked her way back to the Cello Bello and hauled it out. With a squeal, she even found the mop handle with horse hair strings intact, but the handcrafted bow was missing. She thought that Perhaps Daddy took it when he moved away. They decided that since they had the two cars over here that they had the room to haul it back to Lila's barn. They could figure out later what to do with it. Eventually Violet's son might want it for his museum that he talks about. As the pitching and sorting came to an end, Lila stuck her head into the diminishing room and questioned, "No music scores?" Violet slowly shook her head no. Lila said, "Drats!"

Finally they hauled out the trash, boxed up what Violet wanted to keep, and then put back the items that the next family might find interesting. As they were loading the cars, Lila asked Violet if she wanted to stop up to say goodbye to Mrs. Swanson; by now, she would be up from her nap and probably just making her afternoon tea. Violet said she was tired but thought that would be a nice thing to do.

"And it might be my last chance to thank her." Violet's car started up without one gripe. She gave Lila a thumbs-up and followed her up to Swanson's.

Mrs. Swanson met them at the side door, and her eyes brightened when she saw Violet tagging behind Lila. She said, "I thought you were leaving today, so I gave up looking for you. I even made cookies yesterday."

Violet explained that she had car trouble, but she hoped to be on the road by Saturday morning. "Well, come in, come in. I was just having tea and it is already brewed. And some oatmeal cookies. I hope they are all right. You know I don't bake much anymore."

Lila interjected that they could not stay long. While pouring the tea into delicate cups, Mrs. Swanson said, "Violet, I have something for you, that is, if you want them, two beautifully bound books of piano music. There are many compositions by famous composers." She brought them to the table and placed them gently in front of Violet. They were exquisite, and Violet was overwhelmed that she was ready to give them up.

Violet said, "These must have been a gift from someone very special."

"Yes, my music professor at school gave them to me and wrote a lovely message inside the cover."

Violet opened one and it read:

> To a very special person who will be playing in all the famous concert halls someday.
>
> With fondest regards,
> Professor Hanson.

Mrs. Swanson changed the subject by asking, "What do you think might happen to your homestead now?"

Violet said she had no idea. Lila jumped in. "I imagine that now, someone may be able to purchase it quite cheaply and then have enough money to bring it back to livable conditions. It is not as bad inside as one might think by looking at the outside."

"Violet, do you ever imagine yourself buying it and coming back to live here in the valley?"

"Yes, I have imagined that, but it is not possible for me. As they say, life gets in the way."

"I do understand. That happened to me several times."

"Yes," Violet responded, "I just learned today that happened to my mother. I found her teaching certificate down at the house today."

"My goodness, you don't say."

Violet continued, "We were sorting through old records and keepsakes that were stashed away in the small storage room, and I found old letters and cards that I can take back to my son and brother."

"That is such a lovely thing to do."

"I even found Daddy's homemade mandolin."

The comfortable ease that Lila was now feeling with their tea and conversation allowed her to relax a bit and just listen. She originally planned to plant a few more rows in her garden, especially put the corn in; but right now, that did not seem very important. There were plenty of farm markets in the area where she could buy cheap corn, thirteen to the dozen. Violet's visit was running short, and she and Mrs. Swanson were obviously enjoying their repartee.

But Lila was totally surprised when Violet asked Mrs. Swanson, "Have you made any future plans for this lovely home and estate?"

Lila would never have been able to cross that line of familiarity without seeming forward. But Mrs. Swanson showed no offense and, in fact, responded that she had thought about willing it to a good cause such as muscular dystrophy or heart disease. Violet suggested that she might consider breast cancer research. So Lila decided to add a few thoughts of her own.

"I saw an article in my alumni news that the college of arts was thinking about establishing a retreat somewhere in the area where they could foster musicians, artists, writers, and philosophers. This article made me think of the many Chautauqua retreats that were patterned after the original retreat in Chautauqua, New York. The parent retreat in New York is still going strong with well-known speakers, musicians, and artists returning every year."

Now Violet was getting animated. "I remember one that Daddy took us to out in Ohio. We only stopped to listen to a band, guys he knew. But one thing led to another, and before we could say no, we became one of the featured events. We stayed free and played every afternoon on the patio, right outside of the restaurant, became quite popular. Everyone sat on blankets or folding camp chairs and sang along. And Mum, being Mum, was entertaining a group of women with her magic tricks."

Mrs. Swanson decided that Lila should bring that alumni news article next week when she and Benny stop by for his doggie treat.

As they were getting ready to bring this lovely visit to a close, Mrs. Swanson said, "I am so happy that you were able to find all the family things down at the house."

Lila responded, "Not everything. We were looking for Violet's music scores."

"What do you mean by music scores?"

Violet said, "I used to write music with lyrics and hide them because I was afraid to show them to anybody, especially my siblings. They would have poked fun."

Lila added, "Violet hid them, taped to the underside of drawers in a birds-eye maple dresser, but the woman who bought the dresser from the Richards did not find any music there."

"Wait a minute. Did you say the Richards?"

"Yes, there were items that went with the house when it was sold to the Richards. Then Richards sold off the furniture that they could not take with them when they moved."

"Were your scores done on lined yellow tablet school paper??

"Yes, most of them, as that was the only paper I had back then."

"Please, ladies, wait right here. It will only take me a minute."

Open close, open close, clang, bang, snap—finally Mrs. Swanson walked back in and placed a file in front of Violet and asked, "Is this what you were looking for?"

All were speechless. Tick, tick, tick, said the clock on the wall.

Mrs. Swanson broke the ice. "When the Richards closed up, they removed these papers from some furniture which they sold. They dropped it off here, thinking that I would know what to do with this package, being a neighbor and all. I filed it under child music and forgot about it."

Tears were flowing down Violet's cheeks. Lila pinched her cheeks, her favorite trick to keep from crying.

When they drove both cars back home and pulled into the driveway, a deputy sheriff's car was parked in such a way that they had to drive around it to get to Lila's favorite parking space near the house. *"Oscar"*.

When they got out of their respective cars and looked around, Violet said, "Do you suppose he saw us today over at the homestead and he is here, snooping around?"

Lila responded, "With him, anything is possible. Why don't you go on in and put your feet up and I will have a look around."

"Not on your life, I am coming with you."

"Too bad Benny was in the house all day, but then he is not much of a guard dog. Maybe I should get a dog like Marguerite's, huh?"

Lila decided to coax the hens in early with a little chicken feed, but she noticed that Benny went racing on up the path to the bee barn instead of helping with the chickens. Then they heard Benny do several barks and little low growl.

Violet said, "Benny does not sound one bit happy."

They left the chickens scrambling about and headed up the path. Benny had Oscar (Mr. Whitey Tightie) backing up against a tree. Oscar had his hand on his holster, saying, "Whoa, now. Nice dog, whoa." Lila called Benny off.

Oscar growled, "Lady, you need to do something about that dog."

Lila responded curtly, "Maybe that dog doesn't like uninvited busybodies snooping around his property without a search warrant, especially when his mistress is not at home."

All puffed up and hiding his embarrassment, Oscar said, "I am here at the request of the Alma Search and Rescue Department."

"Oh, okay then, may I see your search warrant?"

"I will show you my warrant after you show me your warrant for snooping around in that house over in Goshen."

"Touché. Touché back at you."

Violet now offered, "Let's all calm down, we can talk this out back at the house and work out our differences there." She smiled, and they all started back down the path.

Back on the patio, Lila sat down and offered Oscar a chair, but he preferred the superior standing position. So Violet stood with her arms folded, matching Oscar eye to eye, and said that she believed that he owed Lila an explanation. Lila chuckled inwardly, watching Violet come to her defense, just like old times. Oscar said that the helicopter pilot reported that he saw something over this way, something about a small barn or shack where he saw some activity that made him think we should check it out.

"As you probably know by now, we are looking for an elderly man who seems to be lost, in fact, lost his way going to a doctor's appointment. Now they have recovered his car at the bottom of the Lookout Road. The family suspects a stroke as he has had a small one in the past."

In a lighter mood now, Lila said that if he made his way here, all the way from Bloomsburg, he must have wanted to launch himself into heaven from the summit of Crescent Ridge. Oscar did not chuckle or even smile, so Lila said that they had not seen anyone poking around, but they would be sure to alert the state police if they happen see anybody strange around the bee barn.

As the deputy left, Lila brought out glasses of iced tea and they heard Vinnie pull into the driveway and say, "Hey, Oscar, what brings you over this way?"

Oscar explained again to Vinnie all about his important mission. So the women went on and talked about the day in general and the total surprise about where Violet's music scores were carefully stored away for years. Violet said that she must be losing her touch as she had no prescient thoughts that they ended up with Mrs. Swanson.

Vinnie stepped up on the patio and said, "What's this I hear about some strange man hanging around?"

Lila laughed and said, "Yes, Violet has only been here one week and already strange men are lurking in my driveway, my bee barn, and on my patio."

This brought out a communal chuckle. Violet told Vinnie that it appeared that her car was now roadworthy, but she wanted to test it out on short drives tomorrow and she had a lot of packing and sorting to do. Now she had more things to stuff into her car, so she would have to plead with Lila to store some of the big items which she would not be able to take this time. It was beginning to look like she would not get on the road before Saturday. Anyway it was too late to get to the doctor's appointment this week, so she would have to call and reschedule for early next week. They told Vinnie about all the treasures still loaded in both of their cars.

Vinnie asked, "Did you find the commode?"

Now the mood was lighthearted. Vinnie refused the dinner invitation but said he could stop tomorrow after work to see if Violet needed a hand with anything.

After the hens were safely tucked away for the night and the bee barn was checked out, they made plans for the next day over a little dinner. In the morning, they would reshuffle Violet's heirlooms and family memorabilia and get the most important items packed in first. For the leftovers, Lila said that she had some spare room, here and there, so they would fit it in someplace. Violet suggested that as a test-drive for her car tomorrow that she would drive it over to the homestead for a last look around and perhaps they could have a peek into the barn to see if anything remained that she could remember. She hoped the old hayfork was still there, attached to that center beam—the one that lifted large mounds of hay off the wagon by pulling on several large pulleys and could be swung over to the hay mow and then released. She reminded Lila about their childhood rides on the hay fork; when they could convince one of the boys to work the ropes and pulleys, they used it for launching themselves into the loose haymow. Her older brother was strong enough to pull them both up together.

Lila said, "Remember the time that I landed so hard that it knocked the wind right of me? I thought I heard angels."

Then Violet remembered that there was one more thing she would like to do tomorrow, if there was time. She wanted to get some pictures of the bee barn and the new little bridge that they built so she would have something to show Jimmy and her son when she got back home.

"And there probably wouldn't be enough time but didn't the coal strippings above the maple sugar trees create a large swimming hole which we used for many years? In fact, that was where most of us learned to swim as I remember."

Lila said, "Yes, true, years ago, they were not required to put the land back and plant trees as they have to do by law now."

The raw earth that was exposed after the open-pit mining was simply referred to as the strippings and the large crevices, which filled with water, were called the community swimming holes. Lila went to sleep happy, knowing that they would have a chance to test drive Violet's car one more time before she headed South.

Day 9: Friday

Lila jumped up as soon as George started his usual ruckus. Perhaps when he gets older, he might sleep in just a little bit. She hoped Violet might sleep in but no such luck. Violet called out a good morning and said that she would put the coffee and tea on while Violet went up to the henhouse. Of course, Benny was ready to get his day started. This made Lila think of Marguerite and her dog, Xavier.

"How does one call a large dog with a name like Xavier? You can't say, 'Here, Xavier,' now, can you? I guess if I had actually seen the dog, I would have a better idea how it all worked for Marguerite."

The hens were also anxious to start their day. Benny ran on ahead to the bee barn, but Lila detoured to check the garden before checking the bees. The bees had already started their workday, and out of habit, Lila just peeked inside the bee barn and started back down the path. But halfway back down the path, she thought that something was out of place but not sure what. Oh well, she would check the barn tonight when she went for the night run.

After breakfast, Lila suggested that they bring all items from both cars to her porch where Violet could decide what she wanted to take with her and what could stay here. Then they would have a better idea how to pack the car. When they finished lugging everything onto the porch, Violet began to wonder, what had she been thinking? There was no way that she could get more than half into her car. Lila will not be happy about storing all this stuff. But after she got started and Lila had the idea to break several large boxes down to smaller ones, plus move some nonbreakables into bags, it really did not look so bad. For sure, the sewing machine and some boxes had to stay, but the majority did fit after some stuffing and shoving. Even Bello Cello, when turned right-side up, could be packed with smaller items. She wanted to keep the front seat open until they got back from Goshen today so that Lila could ride with her on the test-drive. This packing and repacking took several hours longer than they had counted on, so they quickly put together a couple of sandwiches and drinks to take along. Just as they started out, Violet asked Lila if she remembered that alumni magazine for Mrs. Swanson, so Lila had to run back into the house and rummage around for it.

On the way to Goshen, they decided that they would have lunch and look around the homestead first because Mrs. Swanson would be napping now. They sat on a large tree trunk which had fallen over near the graveyard and had their lunch. Violet said that her faith made her believe that Niles and Nyla were looking down and smiling. Lila nodded affirmation while inwardly thinking otherwise; however, she could think of no reason to discourage Violet of this comforting thought. Violet would need all the power of positive thinking that she could muster during the next round of therapy. So Lila offered, "And Baby Rose too."

The large barn door would no longer slide but framed into this large door was a smaller-hinged door which they could pry open. The interior was pretty much as expected, only older, and now inhabited by doves having a quiet family conversation with clucks and coos. The smell of ancient hay was still quite strong, but there was no smell now of hooved animals as there had been in the past. The aged and composted manure smelled only of the earth. The hand-powered threshing machine, which was used in another era to separate the wheat grain from the chaff, stood boldly there on ground floor; and with both ladies turning the handle, the inside drum could still be put into action. Violet said Caroline would surely enjoy getting her hands on this museum piece. Using Violet's camera, Lila took some photos of Violet vigorously cranking the handle. They found the two-pronged hayfork up in the haymow where it had fallen from the ceiling beam. The frayed edges of the rope looked to be the work of barn mice, always prevalent with no employed barn cats. They carried the heavy hayfork over and stood it up beside the thresher and took several more photos.

They saw that there were several small holes developing in the roof which would need attention very soon to avoid eventual barn collapse. Lila mentioned that she had heard that you could apply to the state for a grant to restore old barns. She would get the particulars for Caroline. Both Lila and Violet now seemed to be growing comfortable with the possibility that Caroline might be the eventual owner. They closed the barn and walked up to the house, and Violet took photos from the outside but did not want to go inside. With the inside so empty, she just wanted to leave its occupying ghosts at peace. Noting that the time was well past three o'clock, Lila said that it was now safe to stop at Mrs. Swanson's.

Pulling the curtain aside, Mrs. Swanson smiled, slid the lock, and opened the door. She was only slightly surprised to see them and she stepped back offering them entry. "My tea is just brewing so won't you have a cup?"

Violet quickly offered that they would love a cup. Over tea, Mrs. Swanson reviewed the article about the university's quest for a retreat site. She said that she had been giving it a great deal of thought, but she noticed that they wanted to place this retreat in a setting which would offer outside interests such as hiking, boating, and a variety of interesting tours. She did not think that there were many interesting sites in this area. Lila offered that a packed lunch and a guide could take the participants on a day trip up to Crescent Ridge. Mrs. Swanson then remembered the Sunday when her husband had proposed to her at Caleb's Lookout, "Right down on his knee."

Violet piped up. "And a wagon ride to a local apple farm would occupy yet another day." Just then, the amusing story of Uncle Reverend Roland surfaced and Lila thought that Aunt Sue might have her revenge after all. If the retreat offered a boat ride, embarking ten miles northwest on the Susquehanna River and then disembarking at Aunt Sue's landing, then her daughter, Bonnie, could charge an exit tariff. All three ladies had a chuckle over this story. Full of herself now, Lila said maybe the local minister could offer baptism by submersion as well. Praise the Lord!

And Violet offered that Caroline was looking for a larger farm for her riding stable. If she bought her old homestead, she might offer lessons for the retreat participants, for a price, of course. If she ran her fences up to the hardpack road, the sight of beautiful horses running free in a pasture is always alluring.

"And Lila could offer tours to her royal bee farm."

"She has six queens living side by side. Queen Mary, Queen Anne, Queen Elizabeth…"

Lila added, "Queen Eleanor, Queen Catherine de Medici, and Queen Marie Antoinette."

"My goodness," Mrs. Swanson asked, "how did you get three British queens to live harmoniously beside three French queens?"

Lila laughed. "That did take a little planning. I put the powerful Queen Eleanor between Elizabeth and Catherine so she could settle disputes. Queen Eleanor was both a British queen and a French queen and was known for not suffering fools lightly."

Mrs. Swanson, with tongue in cheek, added, "Queen Eleanor gave King Henry quite a sparring good time."

Lila laughed. "And she was very fertile as I need my queens to be."

Mrs. Swanson nodded. "I believe three of her sons were crowned king of England."

Mrs. Swanson was well-traveled, yet they were somewhat surprised at her knowledge of royal history. Violet never had the time nor the inclination to study history.

Sensing their surprise, Mrs. Swanson said she had a wonderful library, thanks to her late husband and that they were welcome to see it, perhaps today, if they had the time.

They both explained that they had some more things on the agenda today, but Lila said that she was very eager to see it, perhaps she could take the time next week when she and Benny came by on their Alma honey run.

It was a tearful goodbye for the two pianists, and Violet asked if she could have Lila take their photo while both were sitting at her grand piano. When seated, they looked at each other and grinned; teasingly, Violet started "Chopsticks" and Mrs. Swanson joined right in. Violet promised to send her a copy of the photo. They gave hugs goodbye. Mrs. Swanson stood on the porch and waved until they drove out of sight and perhaps beyond.

Back home, they walked up to the bridge and took each other's picture. Lila made a light supper while Violet finished packing her car. Lila called out, "Don't forget the mandolin. We put it in the living room last night."

Violet promised her son that she would get a very early start tomorrow morning. While they were having a farewell glass of wine on the patio, Vinnie stopped by, as promised, to see if Violet needed any help. And Caroline stopped by to wish her the best. Violet promised to come back soon and told Caroline that if she bought her old homestead, she may see her more often than she wanted, at least in spirit. Caroline laughed and said she could use an extra hand anytime; it would be a working vacation.

Both women agreed that they had done the best they could with their limited time, and it was best not to stay up all night talking since Violet had a big trip tomorrow and should get an early start.

In Violet's Wake

Day 10: Saturday

The next morning, they shared a quick coffee, tea, and toast. Lila packed a sandwich and snacks for the trip and walked her to the car. Neither one liked long goodbyes, so Violet jumped in, started the car, and drove down the driveway with her ritual waaaaaaaave out the window. After allowing herself a tiny letdown, Lila turned and decided to tend the hens and finish planting the garden, even though it was getting late in the season. She knew that it was best to distract herself with busy work.

By noon, with outside work finished, she sat down on the patio to allow herself time to think through a few things that had been bothering her all during Violet's visit. Interrupting her thoughts, Roger came by to say that the poor lost soul, Buddy, had not been found as of yet and thought he should stop by to warn them. She knew he was just checking to see if Violet had gone South, and she told him that she did. He did not stay long, so Lila went back to her quiet alone thoughts.

Just as Lila walked down to check the mailbox, her neighbors, Jewel and Jack, came walking by hand in hand. Adorable couple; Jack was a skinny guy with a tiny voice box and an Adam's apple which jiggled up and down when he said something which he thought was funny. Jack weighed all of 110 pounds, and Jewel easily outweighed him by seven or eight stones, and she belly-laughed at his stories, no matter how many times she heard it.

Lila smiled, thinking:

> Jack Sprat could eat no fat
> His wife could eat no lean
> So betwixt 'em both
> they licked the platter clean!

Since Lila was feeling the need to fill the Violet void, she invited them up for a cup of coffee and she solicited Jewel's help with the bed jacket she was planning to sew on the Singer to surprise Violet. She also wanted to ask Jack what he had been hearing on his two-way radio police reports. Both Lila and Benny noticed that they did not have their elderly Saint Bernard along. The talk got around to the helicopter flights and the lost man. Jack's Adam's apple started to jiggle, even before he started his story. Jewel gave him a pudgy nudge and he almost spilled his coffee.

In his vibrating guitar string voice, Jack said that yesterday, several Alma police detectives knocked at the door and said they were trying to locate someone who might have come through this area and had they seen any strangers, most likely on foot. Then they said that the helicopter pilot saw someone filling in a large hole which was figured to be just up behind our place. Why yes, Jack told them that he was burying his Saint Bernard.

"Since they were acting mighty suspicious, I told them to go on up and have a look for themselves. 'Well, now,' they sez,' 'you will have to come along and bring your shovel.' Just then, Jewel hefted her mighty weight into their conversation and asked just what were they up to. 'Well, ma'am, your husband is under suspicion of hiding evidence and could be in serious trouble if he doesn't cooperate.'"

Jack said that he would take them to the grave but they could bring their own blankety-blankety shovel. Stretching up all of five foot, two inches, Jewel thought to tell them that the shovel was standing by the backdoor, but they could carry it up there themselves.

In the end, Jewel sent them all up the hill with her mighty arms folded across her chest in her warrior pose. At the gravesite, the deputy sheriff ordered Jack to start digging, if he wanted to clear up this matter. No, Jack said that his mind was quite clear; it was their minds that were clouded. After a short stalemate, the paunchy senior officer took the shovel and started pitching the dirt to the side.

Finally the junior deputy took pity and dug down until the canine fur was exposed. Embarrassed, they took turns shoveling the dirt back into the grave. It was a brisk walk back down the hill where Jewel was waiting, still in warrior pose.

"Sorry, ma'am, just an honest misunderstanding, but one can't be too careful with the crazies running around these days."

"Yes, I see what you mean since we were just visited by two of them."

They jumped into their patrol car and made tracks. Lila asked them if they heard the name Oscar during this conversation.

"Why yes," Jewel said. "The young one was Oscar."

Lila sat there, fascinated with their story and the jiggling Adam's apple. She could not wait to tell Violet.

Around two o'clock, Lila was sitting alone on the patio with a heavy heart when Vinnie stopped by, on his way home from work. He had two Yuengling beers in his hand and a consoling smile on his face.

"Sorry, I don't carry any wine in my cooler."

Lila managed a smile. "Actually a Yuengling brought by a good friend would be just what this lady needs right now. Please join me."

Before sitting, he went into the kitchen and brought out a glass for Lila, knowing that she would not drink straight from the bottle. By nature, neither Lila nor Vinnie were talkative; so they sat quietly and sipped and watched a honeybee sniff at her glass. Finally Vinnie said he thought that she might want some company today. She agreed and said that it was very thoughtful of him to drop by.

"We both are probably feeling her departure."

"You probably more than me," Vinnie replied.

"I remember that you were sweet on Violet years ago."

"Yes, we dated, but her father was always taking the family away somewhere, so there was nothing serious. I am sure you knew that Mr. Stanton kept a very tight rein on both girls."

"Well, actually, no, I didn't. We used to get into all kinds of devilment."

"Mr. Stanton probably trusted you, her serious-minded friend. He probably thought you were at the library. With me, she had to be in by midnight, and if she wasn't, he came looking."

Lila chuckled. "My father used to say there was no need for curfews as one could always do everything one wanted to do before midnight as well as after midnight."

Vinnie laughed. "Smart man."

Vinnie wanted to know how serious Violet's doctor appointments were as she seemed anxious about getting back to Gatlinburg soon.

Lila said, "In all honesty, this is very serious. She has breast cancer and has already had a complete round of radiation and chemotherapy. That worked for some time, but now, the cancer is back and they want to schedule a new round of therapy."

Vinnie asked, "Do you get the feeling that it is terminal?"

With watery eyes, Lila allowed. "Well no one ever knows for sure, but Violet said that hers was of a vicious kind."

Changing the subject, Lila said that she was happy with her new bridge since it was keeping her high and dry, so the railings were purely for aesthetics and photography. "Violet and I went up to snap pictures of each other on the bridge. You should walk up and test it out."

Vinnie reassured Lila that he had not forgotten about the bridge railings. Several construction jobs were taking up a great deal of his time. In most of his jobs, he had to take advantage of the good weather. Lila told him that she had a busy week coming up. For one thing, she had to make a trip over to Brookfield to round up some equipment for Marguerite over in the Hollow.

"Oh, you mean the woman known for her witchcraft brews?"

"We are probably talking about the same woman, but her brews are not witchcraft. Instead they are very carefully handcrafted medicines in her apothecary."

"Do you mean alternative medicine so popular in the magazines right now?"

"Marguerite's elixirs predate the current alternative medicine craze by about three thousand years, originating in Egyptian, Indian, and Chinese cultures."

Vinnie said that perhaps he could use some of her elixirs. "I have been experiencing some joint stiffness each morning. And there is a lot of repetitive motion in construction." To illustrate, Vinnie pretended that he had a hammer in his hand and was tapping it on the table.

"Are you seeing a doctor for that?"

"No, so far, a little exercise each morning seems to take care of it."

"Eventually you may want to see if Mar has something for that, but she won't offer anything if you are already being treated by a doctor. She is wary of drug interactions. And health insurance does not cover her alternative approach."

"Who goes to her then?"

"Those that do not have a doctor or cannot afford a doctor or have become disenchanted with their doctor."

Vinnie also wanted to know if Lila thought Caroline was serious about purchasing and restoring Violet's homestead. Lila thought that it would be a win-win for everyone, and Violet is anxious for her to have it. Lila said that Caroline was very serious about needing more room for her riding academy, and she is well-known for other restoration projects. Maybe the most important point is that she can afford to take on such a large project, especially if her husband approves. "I will invite them to dinner some night so you can have a chance to discuss the project with the two of them."

Looking at his watch, Vinnie said, "I better be on my way, but I wanted to ask if you would like to hike up to Caleb's with me tomorrow?"

Hesitating, Lila said, "Maybe next Sunday instead. Tomorrow I want to hike up to the strippings to check something out up there."

"I would like to tag along. I can check out the maple sugar trees on the way."

Lila smiled. "I hoped you would say that."

"I can be here by 10:30 a.m., if that is okay. I like to sleep in a little on Sundays."

After Vinnie left, it occurred to her that it was time to hear from Violet. She had promised to call as soon as she got home. Lila did a little calculating and decided that it was over the nine hours that Violet needed for her trip home, even with a short stop for gas in Virginia. Immediately the kitchen phone was interrupting those thoughts.

"Hello, Lila here."

"Hello, Violet here."

"Are you home?"

"Record time, it only took me eight hours and fifty minutes, if you subtract the time spent feeding the baby goats."

"Baby goats?"

"When I stopped for gas, there was a guy there who was feeding some baby goats with baby bottles full of milk. I almost bought one for twenty-five dollars, but I did not have the spare cash."

"Why didn't you tell me you were low in cash?"

"Probably best that I didn't. I don't need a baby goat. The guy offered to follow me home to get the cash."

"Now why doesn't that surprise me?"

With Benny, Lila sat there, sorting through the events of the past week. It had been quite a whirlwind of emotions. The one that kept surfacing, however, was that Violet had won Mrs. Swanson over. Now that was one big breakthrough. Lila had been delivering honey for over a year and never got past the side door. In less than one week, Violet and Mrs. Swanson were playing a "Chopsticks" duet. With Violet gone, she was not sure the welcome would last but she hoped that she could continue to pursue the possibility of a Goshen retreat. Then if Caroline could purchase and restore the nearby Stanton homestead, the combined effort would make quite a legacy for the Stantons in general and for Violet in particular. Lila thought it interesting that some people make a lasting impact on the richness of one's life. The names Swanson and Stanton were written in her book.

Lila decided to cook roasted potatoes and a big juicy pork chop on the barbecue grill. She was sad to see Violet go, but she was starving for meat. With the potatoes on low, and the pork chop thawing, she tended to the chickens. Benny, of course, was eager to help. After checking the garden, they took a quick tour to the bee barn. All was quiet. Lila peeked inside and realized what had bothered her yesterday—the other afghan was missing.

The potatoes and pork chop were delicious and satisfying. There was a chill in the air, chasing Lila and Benny inside. She washed the plate, knife, and fork with a little soap on a sponge, rinsed, and stacked in all of two minutes and retired to bed very early with *The Art of Alchemy.* However, she found that alchemy provided very little company tonight. She needed something a bit lighter, so she found some Burns poetry from her mother's collection; that did the trick. She did not want to think about what she had to do tomorrow.

Day 11: Sunday

Lila woke up worried, even before George's challenge; and while the coffee was brewing, she went up to open the henhouse. George gave a hasty rooster jungle call. Over a little breakfast, she mulled over the events of last week: honey jar disturbances, missing items from the bee barn (afghans and flashlight), Henrietta's disappearance, helicopters flying over, Oscar and Roger reporting that a man, known as Buddy, was missing. Also interesting was the report that the helicopter pilot saw some activity around a barn or shack; Oscar claimed that was why he was snooping around the bee barn.

It occurred to Lila that there was an old abandoned foreman's shack up in the strippings. She and her brother use to peek in there and make up stories to scare friends. Lila thought back to many years ago when several hobos took over the foreman's shack. After Father refused Mother's request to run them off, she sent him up with eggs and garden supplies.

Mother said, "Times were hard for a lot of folks, and heaven knows we have eggs and vegetables to spare." Lila thought that she would explain all this to Vinnie on their walk up through the maple sugars trees. *I hope he doesn't think I am being silly.*

While standing on the bridge, Vinnie gave it a B+ with only a minor criticism. He went into detail how the small mistake could be rectified, then he described how he would design the railing so that it would be her most favored site for photos. He even thought that she should make a little clearing for benches and table for a new picnic sight. This made Lila miss Violet even more, but she did not want to think about that right now. She urged him on up the path toward the strippings. But of course, Vinnie had to detour into the maple sugar trees and admire their number and health. As she was encouraging him to stay focused on the way up, she explained why she wanted to come. Finally he stopped and looked at her as though she was a little cuckoo.

Now feeling a little foolish, she said, "Well, it is possible that he may have made his was up to the lookout and then followed the ridge over to here, isn't it?"

"Possible but not likely. Lila, think about it—Caleb's is roughly eight miles away. Not to mention that he had to first hike up to the lookout from his abandoned car."

Lila was thinking that maybe he took the hypotenuse instead of the right triangle, cutting off several miles.

Up and over the first striping embankment, they came to the swimming hole where she had learned to swim after her brother shoved her off his diving rock. She remembered that the shack was just around the next curve and up on a little hilltop, probably positioned there so the job foreman had good views of the coal operation. She had not seen it in years, and it probably was in very poor condition. She noticed that nature had started to reclaim the scarred stripped soil with little trees and dewberry bushes. Vinnie was making little jokes about what they might find. Lila was shushing him to keep quiet.

Just as they came upon the site, they saw a figure skirting behind several trees. With a light touch on Vinnie's arm, Lila restrained him from darting forward. With her heart nearly pounding out of her chest, she called out softly, "Buddy, we are friends. We are here to help you."

No movement and no answer. "Buddy, I am Lila, and this is Vinnie, please let us help you."

Still no answer. "Buddy, your family is worried about you, please let us tell them you are okay."

No movement. Lila and Vinnie started moving ever so slowly toward the shack and stopped again. "Buddy, we won't hurt you, we only want to help."

Vinnie stood there, surveying the decaying shack with broken-out windows. Along the side, he noticed a firepit which had been recently used and what looked a little like chicken bones tossed aside.

After much coaxing, they managed to get Buddy to come with them back down to the house. It took some urging along the way, but they were successful. Lila brought Buddy and Vinnie a warm cup of cocoa out to the patio. Buddy took a skeptical sip and then another. Vinnie sat with him, trying for conversation, but so far—nothing. Lila went into the house and called the Alma Sheriff Department, hoping not to get Oscar on the phone. Being Sunday, no one answered. So she called the state police number and told her story to the officer on duty. He took the address and said he would send someone and could be there within the hour. Lila asked him, if possible, to send an unmarked car and please have no flashing lights which would only scare Buddy even further and he needed medical attention right away. After the nice officer left, promising to get Buddy to the hospital over in Alma, she and Vinnie sat in knee-to-knee silence for a long time.

Finally Lila said, "Thanks, Vinnie, I could not have done that without you."

They discussed the poor man's plight, and Vinnie wondered how he had survived.

"Unknowingly I contributed honey and my favorite laying hen."

"Oh! I did see the chicken bones thrown into the firepit."

"Out of curiosity, I would like to go back up to the shack to see if my afghans are up there. And this time, I can take Benny with me. He would love the exercise."

"I am coming with you. But we should find something to eat before we go."

"I can throw a burger on the grill, now that our vegetarian is safely back in Gatlinburg."

They did find the afghans on the floor of the shack, carefully placed on some evergreen boughs. They also found a pillow which Lila recognized as one she stored up in the bee barn with her sleeping bag. *Strange*, she thought. "I wonder why he did not take the sleeping bag instead of the afghans?"

Vinnie teased, "Probably wanted to dress up his little home here with the latest in design." They remarked on the several holes in the roof and Vinnie said, "Thank goodness it has been dry."

The table and one chair were still intact and looked like it had been used. A roll of paper towels was carefully placed there. Lila told Vinnie that she did keep a supply of paper towels up in the bee barn. And the most astonishing thing was that she spotted her missing fire starter and her flashlight.

"On the night of our hotdog roast, I went into the barn to get this clicker. Could not find it, so I used matches from my emergency supply for lighting the bee smoker. I keep matches in Mother's antique wooden American cheese box, just like she did."

Back down at the house, Lila offered Vinnie a glass of wine as she believed they deserved a little reward. He declined since he had an early date with his construction crew tomorrow morning. Before leaving, he reminded her of their hike up to Caleb's Lookout next Sunday.

Lila went inside, poured a glass of wine, pulled out the ingredients for Dave's coffee cake, and started a little supper. Cake in the oven, she sat with her wine, went back over the day's events, and forgot to eat. She would have to tell Violet that she was onto something when she wanted to hunt for Henrietta further up into the strippings. *What is this gift she possesses? Is it possible? Perhaps if I had told Violet my concerns about the missing items from the bee barn, she would have made the connection to Buddy much faster than I did. Violet was always at the conclusion first, waiting for me to get there. Possibly she just has more neurotransmitters, so she can think faster. How I miss her, let me count the ways!*

Benny started to fuss and fidget, reminding Lila that they had chores. Jumping up from her reverie, Lila remembered the hens. She laughed. "Benny, I think you are related to Violet."

At the henhouse, Lila almost shed a tear for Henrietta; but no, she stopped that nonsense. Henrietta may have saved a man's life. After chores were done and next week's schedule was planned, she called it a day. As she climbed into bed, she wished she had made some of that turmeric tea. She would stop in Alma tomorrow for turmeric.

Day 12: Monday

To Lila's relief, there was a lovely garden-watering shower overnight and the morning sun had not yet burned off the haze. She was hustling around to make the trip to Brookfield today. She had been asked to come in for a consultation about a drug development she had been working on when she took her leave. The project was put on the back burner when she left, but now, the new supervisor wanted to reactivate it. And Lila also wanted to search around in the storage closets for equipment.

Benny and Lila hurried up to let the hens out and check water and grain pans. Since she would be gone all day, she decided that is was too lovely today to keep Benny inside the house, so she also checked his water and food bowl. His doghouse was purchased second-hand at a moving sale several years ago, when elderly neighbors had to move in with their daughter, and she placed it in a shady spot on the patio near the entry door. A sign painted above the doghouse door read, "Guard Dog on Duty." She thought the sign was clever, but at the time, she did not believe that Benny would really do much guarding. Recent events had her thinking otherwise. When the telephone rang, she almost decided not to answer but reconsidered. It was Buddy's daughter.

"Are you the lady that found my dad?"

"Well, yes, along with a friend."

"I want to thank you and tell you that we will be bringing him home today, that is, home to our hospital here. Since he did not get immediate help for his stroke, I am afraid he is in for a long recovery."

"I am very sorry to hear that. Perhaps you will keep me informed."

"My husband and I would like to visit you some day this week to thank you properly, and perhaps, you could show us where you found him."

"Looking at my schedule, I am free on Friday or Saturday."

"We both work, so Saturday would be perfect for us."

"Bring your hiking clothes and shoes if you want to see Buddy's hideaway."

The trip to Brookfield was a pretty mountainous drive; some of the shady mountain laurels were still hanging onto their blooms. The streams were still full of themselves, rushing to the Susquehanna as though there was some race to get there. For part of the trip, she could have taken the expressway, but Lila needed this restorative time to enjoy the scenery. She reminded herself that the reason that she took this leave was to enjoy a few of these moments. After her husband died, the chemical research world lost some of its luster, at least for now.

At the plant, not much had changed on the exterior grounds, except someone had made a picnic area under the large red oak tree which she planted ten years ago, in memory of her husband. She just hoped that she did not bump into Harold; he held a grudge about some incident in the past. The current supervisor asked her if she could take some time with a new young fellow by the name of Adeeb Guyesudin who had taken over one of her research projects. Throughout the introductions, she could not help but notice that the new researcher looked at her peculiarly, as if she did not meet his expectations. Also she noticed that he was startlingly handsome for someone stuck away in a laboratory. Her husband would have joked that someone went crazy in the casting department. Anyway she sucked in her breath and gently pursued how he was progressing with the project. After the initial hesitations, together they warmed to the subject and spent the morning interpreting results and making suggestions, especially about the buffering solutions that were employed in the sample separations.

For lunch, they took cafeteria food out to the picnic area, and the new research fellow revealed that he was from Pakistan and had spent a lot of time studying in England. Lila learned that he was an overachiever with both an MD and a PhD. Lila jokingly called him Doctor-Doctor Guy, and he said that most people here did shorten his name to Guy.

He was a charming young man with an Omar Shariff smile. She resisted the urge to call him Omar instead of Adeeb. He missed his wife who stayed back in England with her own counseling business. With encouragement from Lila, he talked about the adjustments he was making here in Brookfield; he liked to cook but was finding it difficult to find the right spices for his native dishes, but his wife often sent some by mail. He had heard about a store in Sutton, called Old World Spice Shop, that carried spices from many foreign places. That was welcome news for Lila who said that she would love to see that shop since she was now helping an alchemist who ordered various spices by mail.

As they were gathering up their trays, Harold came sauntering up to the table and said that he wanted to say hello. They were deferentially polite to each other but not exhibiting any warm emotions. She still had the notion that he sabotaged the tertiary testing of Drug Program XI. He may have been exacting revenge for being passed over for a promotion; Lila had recommended Sylvia for that promotion and he probably knew who made that recommendation. Still she was not completely certain, but the way he skulked around after most had gone home for the night made her suspicious. And their lab doors were often unlocked with the last to leave charged with the duty of locking.

In the afternoon, she went to the storage room, looking for instruments and equipment which Marguerite might be able to use. Everything she needed was there and already out-of-date and probably headed to the recycling bin, so the supervisor told her to take whatever she wanted.

"And by the way," he said, "if your alchemist has any plant product we might be interested in, especially immune-response catalysts or inhibitors, please let us know."

Lila told him that she had not made real inroads yet into any of her special formulas, but she hoped to get her help with a skin moisturizer that she was experimenting with at home. "We are not in the beauty business, but good luck with your cottage industry."

Lila told him that perhaps he should think about it as the beauty industry was a billion-dollar business with not many lawsuits.

He agreed that she did make a good point and he sent a young lab tech to help her haul equipment to her car. Not wanting to miss an opportunity, she stopped to see a few old friends before heading home. On the way home at dusk, she started to worry about the hens still outside, and she figured that Benny was worried about her.

When Benny did not run out from the doghouse to greet her, she wondered if he had run back into the house when she left; perhaps he was trapped inside. She went inside to check but no response. She called upstairs and roamed through the house to double-check. Still no Benny. She changed her shoes and walked outside, glancing around with a flashlight since it was nearly dark now. As she walked up to the henhouse, she saw Benny stationed in front of the open door, looking all expectant about something. Flashing the light inside, all eight hens were settled in for the night, clucking among themselves.

"Wow, Benny, you never cease to amaze me. What a good boy!"

She flashed the light up to George's roost, but he just turned his head away from the light. She latched the door and headed back down to the cottage. Lila was really missing Violet now since she was the only person who would believe this Benny story. But then again, maybe she could tell Caroline who has probably seen more unusual animal traits than anyone else. Benny was anxious to come into the house and enjoy Lila's company and get a few expected doggie treats. Lila made a bowl of shredded wheat and now, allowing herself to feel tired, she retired.

Day 13: Tuesday

After chores, Lila whipped up a batch of her face cream that she wanted to take over to Marguerite's today, that is, if she was allowed to come this afternoon after finishing work at Jed's. She was nearly satisfied with her recipe but felt that it was missing some important ingredients. At Jed's, it was nice to see most things were back to normal. Sonny's pickup was not there, but he was inside acting the star. Everyone was signing his full leg cast with great flourishes; even Rachel's gang was getting silly and signing with colored markers. Burt signed it "Stay away from Dead Man's Curve or there may be flowers and a cross the next time. Ha, ha." Coaxed by Burt, Lila finally agreed to sign, "Sonny, a great guy who broke his leg just to get attention."

Marguerite had the potatoes peeled and she was cleaning and chopping the vegetables that Jed needed for a stir-fry today. Lila started in gently and said that she could follow her home today if that suited her schedule. Marguerite nodded. She told her that she was able to get some equipment at Brookfield Chemical which she thought Mar could use, but only if she wanted to. Marguerite nodded.

"Marguerite, we will go carefully and thoughtfully before we replace any of your equipment. I will help you make changes, but only if you want to make them. I think some of the changes will make your life easier."

As Lila followed Marguerite up her driveway, she had her first look at Xavier. "Yikes! He is big, just as Jed said."

Wisely, she waited with the windows firmly closed. Xavier made a quick full circle around her car and jumped up to have a look, eye to eye, through the glass window. Lila didn't move but managed to look at him and smile. She was wondering if he knew what a smile meant. She was thinking that Violet should be here, she would know which smile to use. Marguerite got out of her car and Xavier ran over for his pat on the head. Then she signaled Lila to stay put; she needn't worry about that. Dog and owner disappeared into the cabin. Then her little head appeared at the backdoor and she motioned for Lila to come in.

Lila began by bringing in just the water-bath incubator because that would probably be the one item that Marguerite could accept most quickly. And she was right, the ancient one she had tried to repair had already been removed. Lila slipped the new one in and explained that she would have much better control with the sliding temperature control. Next she wanted to know if she could bring in the hot-air incubator and the emulsifier, and Marguerite nodded okay. This was turning out easier than Lila had expected, but she knew that the centrifuge would offer a steeper learning curve.

Marguerite said that she preferred natural sedimentation methods over man-made centrifuges. But Lila countered that she would have more control in separating different density materials if she was willing to try it.

"You know your grandparents made improvements on the ancient methods as better equipment became available."

This seemed to take hold with Marguerite. Lila said, "I can demonstrate it, and you could then make up your mind later. It would not hurt to try it."

After the demonstration, time and energy were winding down. Lila knew it would be a several-hour project to even broach the subject of replacing the alembic, let alone teaching her how to use modern distilling equipment, so she suggested that they postpone that until Thursday. Marguerite seemed to be relieved by that prospect and she asked Lila if she wanted to take a moment in the butterfly garden before she left.

Day 14: Wednesday

Today, Lila woke up early as she was anxious to get the honey extraction done. She had thirty frames of honey that she wanted to extract by centrifugation. After centrifuging, she used large-pore filters so that most of the healthy ingredients were still included in the raw honey. She fine-filtered a few jars for those who insisted on honey that would be heated and pasteurized. Honey extracting is demanding but rewarding labor when one realizes that each worker bee flies many miles per day just to gather the nectar to produce only a few drops of honey. The glass jars were washed and ready and the labels made: "Raw Honey, Lila's Bee Farm." She wanted to make a sign to post down by the mailbox that read, "For Sale: Raw Honey and Free-Range Chicken Eggs."

After the home chores were done, Lila and Benny headed over to Goshen so that they would arrive after Mrs. Swanson's nap time. Mrs. Swanson was expecting them. Lila told Benny that he had to wait on the porch, but no—even he was invited in. They had tea and Benny had his homemade doggie biscuit; and then, unexpectedly, Lila was invited into the library. Over the years of her education, Lila had seen several university libraries, so she did not expect to be overwhelmed by a home library. But this library was quite extraordinary. It held several collectible archives in art, science, and history and many with gilt edges.

Obviously it had been quite a source of pride for the family. Mrs. Swanson said that they always brought back at least one rare book when they traveled. There were more first editions here than held at some of the major book repositories. It probably did not rival Monticello, but it was special for a little Goshen home library. Mrs. Swanson figured that she should bequeath the collection, but she did not know to whom or where. This idea had Lila stumped, but she said she could research possibilities. Once again, Lila had the realization that because of age differences, many relational opportunities are lost. How great it would have been to have known her when she and Violet were roaming these hills on their bicycles. Instead of peeking in her windows, they could have been benefiting from this extraordinary woman's knowledge.

Left alone in the library to browse, she found a book on flowering plants with a picture of the plant known as giant hogweed which looked somewhat like wild parsnips. This really caught her attention since Lila received a small printed notice, sent to her by Bevin Bee Supply, announcing that importing of this plant was banned in New York and Pennsylvania. Beekeepers had coveted this plant due to its overly large flowering heads that honeybees really liked. It went on to say that this plant was becoming quite invasive near our streams and waterways, taking over natural habitat and rooting out native plants. And that the leaf sap was phototoxic, causing severe skin rashes, burns, and blisters with long-term consequences.

Apparently in the nineteenth century, hogweed was introduced into New York gardens for its showy flower head and its magnificent height. When corralled within these garden boundaries, it did not create a problem. But as usual, it was propagated and spread both by nursery suppliers and eager folks, simply snitching a few seeds and then moved into other flower beds across the state until it escaped from confined areas and settled into the wetlands of New York and

Pennsylvania where it flourished only too well. Now there is an area-wide plea to help eradicate this plant.

Mrs. Swanson's book stated that the correct name for giant hogweed was *Heracleum mantegazzianum* and was described as Queen Anne's lace on steroids. Lila noticed that the genus name was probably referring to Hercules and the very appropriate species name was probably humorously adopted for the plant because it could grow eighteen feet tall in the best wet habitats; however, it usually maxed out at twelve to fourteen feet tall. It is often confused with three other closely related plants, cow parsnips, angelica, and Persian (common) hogweed, all slightly toxic, but one can discern the difference by the purplish spotted hairy stem of giant hogweed, plus some other distinguishable features of the leaves. Persian hogweed is native to the Middle East and apparently not invasive there. In Iran, they crush the seeds to produce the spice, *golpar*, an alternative to cardamom which is used to flavor vegetable dishes.

Interrupted by a very light tap on the door, Lila looked up to see Mrs. Swanson pushing a small tea cart prepped with a teapot, cups, and biscuits, both human and doggie.

"Ahh, how lovely, you must have found something nice to read."

"Yes," Lila replied. "This book has helped me immensely. I now have an idea what giant hogweed looks like. I seem to remember a song about the "Return of the Giant Hogweed," sung by a popular band about ten years ago. You know, the young-kids type of music."

Mrs. Swanson smirked. "You call that music?"

Lila laughed. "I will have to ask Violet who the so-called artists were."

Pouring tea, Mrs. Swanson said, "A man from the state environmental agency came around, asking if I had any hogweed or gooseberries growing on the property. I said I didn't think so."

"Oh gee," said Lila, "I hope he doesn't find my gooseberries. Whatever is wrong with having gooseberries?"

Mrs. Swanson said, "The currant and gooseberry plants are the alternate host in the life cycle of the white pine rust fungus. So they are trying to interrupt the cycle."

Lila suggested, "Perhaps we should get rid of the white pine instead." Then she said, "Whoops, I may have offended you. I know you are part of a timbering family."

While pouring tea, Mrs. Swanson laughed and said, "I was always fond of gooseberry pie myself. Anyway anytime the state gets involved with eradication, we often end up with unintended results. Lila, why don't you take that book as a gift from me? I won't have need of it."

Gently closing the book, Lila stirred a little lemon and honey into her tea and leaned back for a silent moment before replying. Finally she said that she was grateful for the offer, but she thought it best if all the books remained here, in this library, until the decision had been made on how her estate was to be handled. If she willed it to the university for a study and educational retreat, these books would greatly augment that effort.

However, if she willed the estate to a not-for-profit agency, uninterested in books, then she would probably want to hire an appraiser and get advice on how best to sell or donate the library for further study somewhere. After a little give-and-take on ideas, Mrs. Swanson asked Lila if she would like to initiate the conversation with the agency at the university that was mentioned in the alumni news. Lila said that she could probably take on the initial conversations, but they would soon need legal advice if and when talks proceeded past the fact-finding stage. Benny and Lila took their leave, promising to stop by again next Wednesday.

Lila had hoped to step into the very small library in Rockton, but it was past closing time so she would try for a visit some other time, later this week; she wanted to see how the renovations were proceeding. A generous donor had given the library a large sum of money, so they could add a new wing which would house more books and a meeting room. The library building had been one of the original houses along Main Street, so it had a prime location with room for growth. Vinnie was donating several benches for the flower garden located just to the side. He lost the bid on the main construction because a large firm in Alma had underbid him. However, he wanted to donate the benches in memory of his father who had helped the library with the first remodel of the original structure.

Pulling into her driveway, she noticed Samuel pedaling his bicycle down the road at breakneck speed, reaching her car door just as she stopped. She had not seen him all winter and she had missed his little visits. Last fall, Samuel told Lila probably more than she was supposed to know. Apparently his mother decided that he had surpassed her so greatly that she did not feel qualified to homeschool him any longer. And even little Rebekah, two years younger, was beginning to campaign to be allowed to matriculate with him. There were many very quiet past-bedtime discussions which both children could patch together, listening through the floorboards from their loft. Father was worried that it would taint Samuel's ways and he would start thinking too many worldly thoughts and aspirations. On the other hand, Mother seemed to think that he might revolt and they would lose him altogether. In the end, Mother won the day and they allowed him a trial year at the public school.

"Samuel, I missed our visits. How are you?"

Removing his black-brimmed hat, he said, "Very well, ma'am. Finished my first year at Rockton Elementary. Next year, I will be going over to Alma Junior High."

Stepping out of the Jeep, Lila said, "That's wonderful, so nice to hear. How did it go?"

"Well, I had a ragged start, what with my funny clothes and all."

"And how did that work out?"

"Mrs. Cruikshank sat us all down and asked us to name as many types of dogs that we could. After she listed twenty or so types on the board, she asked if we had a favorite. But she said, of course, she just knew that we all would love to have exactly the same type of dog, that we all would want the cute floppy-eared beagle. Well, there was such a howl that went forth, each claiming to prefer their own pet over the beagle. 'My dear students, this is called diversity. God never intended for us to like the same things, dress exactly alike, or even to like the same foods. Life would be one big boring bad dream if each of us looked identical, had the same teeth, eyes, hair, and wore the same clothes.'

"After a moment of silence, Jerry, the class clown, said, 'That would be okay if everyone was as handsome as I am.' That, of course, led to boos and shouts."

Lila asked, "What happened next?"

"I raised my hand and said that I had a pet llama, his name is Albert. And I know he likes diversity because his closest friend is a pig named Dixie."

Lila was thinking that she would make an effort to meet Mrs. Cruikshank.

Once again, Lila had put in an overly ambitious but fulfilling day. She called Violet after chores and supper to bring her up to date with Mrs. Swanson's intentions. Also she regaled her with Benny's intrepid guarding of the henhouse story. Violet suggested that Benny should be taught how to close and latch the henhouse door so he could relax and get back down to the house before dark. This made them both laugh.

Violet said yes, she remembered the giant hogweed song and thought the band was Genesis, but she would ask her son about it. Lila learned that Violet was scheduled to start chemotherapy on Monday, so she may not be in touch for a while since the treatment always made her feel wrung out and nauseous. Lila went to bed feeling a little southern cloud of melancholy wafting overhead, making her skin feel cold. Violet was her touchstone.

Day 15: Thursday

Again after the prep work at Jed's was finished, Lila followed Marguerite home and waited for Mar to call Xavier into the cabin. She then brought in the parts to assemble a distillation apparatus that would replace the antique and crumbling alembic. She knew this was a very sensitive issue, being a wide divergence in historic methods; but if she could get her to try it, she knew Marguerite would believe that it was truly better for many reasons, including reliability and control. She would not mention speed as that was not important to Mar.

It took the better part of the afternoon to get the rigging just right due to shape and size constraints, but she did have it set up and operational by late afternoon. She then taught Marguerite how the controls worked and asked her for a sample—any sample—that she wanted to distill and condense down through the coils. She set up three separate collecting flasks because she noticed that there were three attachment ports on the old alembic. She had to guess where to set the graduated cooling temperatures, but for this demonstration, it was not extremely important. Marguerite would not divulge exactly what she was distilling. The important thing was for Marguerite to see how the process worked. From the expression on Mar's face, she could see that the new equipment made an impression. Again she said that if after trying it on her own and she did not want it, Lila could take it back and perhaps see if her antique alembic could be repaired or rebuilt. Lila left a recipe and a sample of face-hydrating cream and asked Marguerite if she would mind looking it over sometime.

After she got home and just as she sat down to a little sandwich and a soothing tea, chamomile, turmeric, cinnamon, and honey, Dr. Guy called and apologized for calling at dinnertime. He had some unexpected results that he wanted to discuss with her. Apparently he could not repeat the results that he showed her on Monday and could he come over to Rockton this weekend and bring his printouts. Lila said she had appointments this weekend but perhaps she could travel to Brookfield next week. In the meantime, she told him to recheck the pH of his buffers because that had happened to her in the past; she was sorry to say this, but she suspected foul play.

"I would advise you to change the door locks on your lab, get new keys, and only give a copy to your lab tech and to the supervisor. If both you and your tech go to lunch at the same time, lock the door. Always recheck the buffers immediately before each individual experiment."

Day 16: Friday

Lila wanted to straighten and clean the house and the bee barn. After the whirlwind honey extraction the other day, there was equipment to be cleaned, jars to be labeled and wiped of dripped honey. Since Buddy's daughter was scheduled to come tomorrow, she also thought that it might be nice to take the afghans back up to the shack today so that it looked at least semi-inhabitable and not so forlorn for them to see it for the first time. After all, the shack was quite a sight with its rotting roof and broken windows. She did not know whether she should remove the chicken bones or not. Well she would decide that after she got there. Vinnie may want to come along when Buddy's family came and then skip their hike on Sunday. Sometimes he is finished by noon on Saturdays. And with all these trips up and down to the shack, she thought her thighs were getting plenty of exercise. Also she wanted to fix ahead something nice for tomorrow's luncheon.

After cleaning and cooking, Benny and Lila trudged back up to the strippings and laid the afghans back into the shed, the same way Buddy had placed them—carefully as though he was making his bed each morning. This made Lila think that this was a man careful about his surroundings. After she tidied up just a tiny bit, she looked around and thought that it did not look too bleak for Buddy's daughter to see. She decided to leave the firepit just as Buddy left it, with the chicken bones and all. This would help explain how her father had cleverly survived his ordeal. This thought made her wonder if he could recover from his severe stroke. It certainly had not affected his survival skills nor his desire to live.

On the way back down, Benny went chasing after something that only dogs can sniff out, so she continued down by herself, knowing he could find his way home. He knew these woods even better than she did. As she sat down on the bridge and thought about how nice it would be to have the fancy railing that Vinnie had talked about, Benny came whimpering onto the bridge.

"Come here, Benny, what did you get into?" As he guiltily came forward, she took a closer look. "*Oh no*! Benny! Didn't you learn your lesson from several years ago? You are smart enough to let porcupines alone. Well, let's get down to the house and get those quills pulled out before the swelling and infection gets started."

After pulling the quills and dressing his wounds, she received a call from Caroline checking on Violet's status since she had not heard. Lila apologized for not keeping her updated. After telling her about Benny's encounter with a porcupine, Caroline said she would drop off a homemade salve that she uses when her horses get infections around their hooves. Lila agreed that would be nice.

Since it was now after dinnertime, she thought she would call Vinnie to see if he wanted to hike up to the shack tomorrow when Buddy's family came. Vinnie decided that he could probably get there in the afternoon to meet the family, but she should go ahead on the hike without him. He had to finish up a job tomorrow morning. Lila mentioned that they could skip the Sunday hike up to Caleb's Lookout if they went back up to the strippings tomorrow.

"No way, we have a date for Sunday as promised."

Day 17: Saturday

The day started out rainy and cool, making Lila think that they might call and cancel the trip since she had warned them that it was quite a long hike up to Buddy's hideaway. But she was ready with a coffee cake and fruit for when they arrived. She looked around and the cottage looked good enough for company. After chores, she put in time until the guests arrived. Finally Patty and Mike arrived with two inquisitive grandchildren, worried about their favorite Pop-Pop. After all the thank yous were extended and a bite of coffee cake eaten, they were anxious to get started. The weather was clearing and the temperature now perfect for a hike. Lila said she could answer their questions on the way up as she was sure there were many. She said she should have put two and two together quicker, but she had been distracted with company. The first question was how he could have made his way over here from where his car was parked. Lila said she had a theory that may be better explained when they had a better view from up above.

Anxiously she tried to prepare them for what they would see at the top and was secretly glad that she replaced the afghans in the shack. The shock of seeing what Buddy had endured was going to be heart-wrenching. When the shack came into view, they all stopped in stunned silence. Lila hurried up to tell them that unlike this morning, the weather had been mostly clear and mild for the last two weeks. When they got to the firepit and stopped to investigate, Lila realized that it would have been better to have removed the chicken bones, but it was too late now. They would need an explanation.

As they stooped down, picking up chicken bones, Lila said, "I am happy that I had something that he knew how to cook."

As his daughter stepped inside and asked, "Where do you suppose he got those pretty covers?"

Lila, after waiting for the light to dawn, put the best spin on his plight, telling them that they were some old covers which she had in that little barn which they passed on the way up. When they looked at her in amazement, she said, "Everybody has a right to survival. That was all he was doing, and I am glad that these few things helped him."

After they all had a chance to thoroughly investigate Buddy's shack, Lila led them on a short hike up to a small promontory where they had a view across a ridge and up to another peak called Caleb's Lookout. She admitted that she really did not know how far it would be to walk around the ridge, but the helicopter pilot could give them an estimate. "Of course, he had to walk up to the lookout first if he came across the ridge. More than likely, he cut off miles by walking up through that valley there and turning diagonally up this way. We will probably never know for sure."

They then wanted to get pictures of the shack to show friends where Buddy survived his ordeal, and they hoped Lila would pose for one or two.

On the way back down, they talked nonstop, speculating on how it all happened and how Buddy put in the time without his books. Lila learned that he had been a history major and had been a curator at a small museum for many years. His wife died several years ago, so he was used to taking care of himself, probably contributing to his survival over the past two weeks.

Back down at the bee barn, she showed them where he found the old covers, and she admitted, a little honey as well. By now, they allowed themselves a little chuckle. Lila gave them a jar of honey for Buddy when he came home from the hospital. She coaxed them to stay for a little lunch as it was already prepared. Vinnie arrived just as they sat down, so now, new questions were addressed to him. In the late afternoon, they left, promising to keep Lila posted on Buddy's progress.

Lila gave Vinnie a detailed report about the hike up and back down. Vinnie said he was proud of her for following through with her suspicions. Getting ready to leave, he told Lila that he would pick her up tomorrow for their hike around 10:30 a.m. and that he would bring the snacks.

As Lila was getting ready for bed, the doorbell rang; it was Caroline, apologizing for coming so late. She explained that she just got back from Harrisburg where she went to petition the board of the state horse show to include handicapped riders into one of their summer venues. They liked her ideas and were willing to consider giving her a time slot to showcase her special students. She felt the thrust of this venue should show how riding helped the disadvantaged in all categories. She would have to make several trips yet to work with a committee that dealt with such issues. She knew that some of her star pupils would be willing to take part in this event. Transporting her special horses was not a problem, but she knew her biggest issue would be solving transportation and housing of the students while there.

The board said that she would have to figure out the financial end of that herself, but they would schedule in the time for this event. Lila suggested that there was an RV dealer over in Alma who might be convinced to let her rent a large RV that would accommodate, transport, and house the students right on the grounds while there. If the dealer could be convinced that this was great for PR, he might give her a special deal.

Caroline said, "Hmm…Maybe."

Then Caroline popped open her trusty apothecary case which she carried with her everywhere for treating her horses and dogs for all kinds of infections, rashes, and ailments. She only calls the vet for problems beyond her ken. Lila had pulled the porcupine quills from Benny's tender nose and treated with an antiseptic lotion, but several sites were beginning to redden and swell.

Caroline looked through her case and recommended a salve that she thought could work, one she uses on her horses when they get into pasture nettles and briers. Benny was willing to allow Caroline to examine his sore nose after she used her other voice—the soothing one that said, "I am the nurse here and I know what to do."

Watching Caroline, Lila was thinking that this small community was full of medical knowledge that came from a variety of sources. Marguerite's came from generations of alchemists, and Caroline's came from generations of farmers and ranchers. She was wondering if someone should update the *1919 Encyclopedia of Medicinal Preparations*, but then someone probably has already done so somewhere. Maybe she could investigate that on her next visit to the Alma Library.

Caroline said it was too late tonight, but on a better day, she wanted to talk about Violet's homestead. Her husband was supportive of the project, if she could get it for a reasonable price and the restoration didn't cost too much; but she knew that Lila was hoping Violet would come back to live. Lila told her that she was not the gatekeeper on who owned what around here, but it looked certain that Violet has no desire to return, except to visit.

"And it is not only health related," she added. "Violet has spread her wings under a warmer sun. She would be happy to know that you had the property as she feels confident that you would do a proper restoration. If you would like, I will have you and your husband come to dinner some night when Vinnie is free. He would be able to give you some tentative costs for the kinds of projects you would need done." Caroline was very interested for Lila to put this together, and she would bring the dessert.

"Okay, Benny, it is time to call it a night, it has been an extraordinary day. One we won't forget. anytime soon." Benny, already in his bunk, did not lift his ointment-covered nose, but he did lift one ear just to acknowledge that he was listening.

Day 18: Sunday

After hurrying home from church, Lila was changing into hiking clothes and rummaging around, looking for the binoculars which she had forgotten to take when she and Violet went up to the lookout. Noticing the time was 10:30 a.m., she was expecting Vinnie anytime. And sure enough, Vinnie arrived and she yelled down, through an open window, that she would be right down.

"No problem, take your time."

She was berating herself for not keeping her binoculars with her hiking equipment. Just then, she heard another car down on the road, coming to an abrupt stop, backing up, and pulling into the driveway. Through the front upstairs window, she could see that it was the Alma News truck. A very young reporter and cameraman got out and came to the door. Vinnie answered and she heard Vinnie say, "No, Lila is not home right now, probably gone all day, perhaps you can call tomorrow."

She was not sure how she felt about him making that decision for her, but if she took the time now to answer their questions, they would miss the best time of the day to reach the top. So she would let that one slide for now.

The weather was warming, but they dressed in layers which could be peeled as necessary. Benny was feeling a little better today, so she decided the hike would be good for him as well. No other cars were in the parking lot, so it looked like they had the trail to themselves. She laughed, telling Vinnie about the elderly couple who bested her and Violet up and down. They stopped for water at the halfway sitting rock and looked for carved initials; and sure enough, there was Vinnie's and his high school sweetheart, Jo-Jo's.

"Lost that one," he said.

Lila remembered the car accident that took Jo-Jo's life. Vinnie said he wanted to look for Lila's boyfriend's initials. "Not here," she said, "Never had a boyfriend until college. High school boys were afraid of bookish girls. At least, I like to think that was why I never had a date for the prom."

When they got to the top, they sat down for more water. Lila gave Benny a drink from a paper cup. Rummaging his backpack, Vinnie offered the first round of snacks. Lila looked over the landscape, and with binoculars, she could make out the roof of Violet's homestead, peeking through the trees. She told him that the other day, she was not sure but the Swanson estate was easily discernible without binoculars. He took his turn looking through the glasses.

She decided to tell Vinnie some of their childhood stories and about the grand piano and what it meant to Violet. And then she moved up to the possibility of Mrs. Swanson donating her estate for a retreat. She thought that would fit right in if Caroline bought Violet's homestead for her riding academy. Growing restless, Vinnie finally said that he had something he wanted to discuss. Lila knew he was quieter than usual on the hike up. He was never very talkative, but today, he did seem concerned about something.

"I am thinking about asking Jillian for a divorce."

"What? You mean you are not divorced?"

"No, we never got around to it."

"How many years have you been separated?"

"Going on six now."

"Do the ladies that you are dating know that you are not divorced?"

"None of them ask."

"Don't you think it is possible that the reason you never divorced is that you both thought you might reconcile someday?"

"Probably true in the early stage, but it is far too late for that now."

"Well, as a friend, I recommend strongly that if you do file for divorce, that you stay away from all romantic relationships, not even friendly dating until things are final. You never know how a woman will feel about being tossed aside for a new love. A spurned woman could make things quite messy."

Vinnie went silent and decided to look through the binoculars and discuss how he thought Buddy, a possible stroke victim, might have worked his way over to the strippings. Lila was sure that unless they could see Buddy's home landscape, they would probably never know what the poor soul was thinking. He would have taken a route that reminded him of going home. Vinnie swung around to Coal Hill to see if he could spot the outcropping near the shack. Lila suggested that they should plant a white flag up there so that they could spot it from here. Vinnie brought out the second batch of snacks. Lila's thoughts returned to the conversation at hand.

"Was it Violet's visit that started this divorce thinking?"

"Well, in a way, but not in the way that you are thinking. Her visit made me see things in a whole different light."

"Vincent, you are talking in riddles!"

"Are you going to make me say what I am afraid to say?"

"I am afraid that I won't understand unless you make yourself very clear."

"It was easy to see that Violet adores you, you are her anchor."

After careful thought, Lila said, "Violet is a very special person, and I am not sure she needs an anchor. She knows how to soar, but she always knows where to land."

"Lila, that may be true, but to my way of thinking, you are the special one."

After a long pause. "Now you are forcing me to say what I must say. I will never allow myself to be the cause of a divorce. You should only get a divorce if it is the right thing to do."

"Are we at an impasse?"

"Yes, I am afraid we are."

Vinnie extended his hand. "Still friends?"

"Yes, still syrup-and-honey friends." Lila took his hand in both of hers.

The view from Caleb's is magnificent and it also has a way of cleansing the air.

Five Minutes of Fame

As Lila was just finishing the chores up at the bee barn, she heard a vehicle crunching the gravel as it turned up into her driveway. She called hello as they were getting out of the truck, camera and notepads at the ready. The news reporter, identifying herself as Jill and the cameraman as Brad, asked if this was a good time to talk about Buddy and where he was found; she had heard that it was in a shack on this property. Lila felt a little nervous when the cameraman started filming, so she asked him to shut down the camera until they had a chance to discuss some privacy issues. After thinking things over last week, she realized that this story could have the potential to make curiosity seekers troop up past her house and on up the trail to sleuth out the shack. On the one hand, it might be fun to be "The Woman Who," but on the other, it would bring unwanted traffic through her property.

Lila said that she would come into the studio for a question-and-answer session, provided that they guaranteed that her address was not revealed. And it would have to be arranged when Vinnie could attend the interview as well. Jill was not very happy with these parameters and kept nudging her way past Lila and peering on up in the direction of the bee barn. Lila turned and walked back down to the news truck and opened the passenger door, then stepped back. The reporter, probably just doing her job, called over her shoulder that it looked like a shed and not a shack; what she was seeing really at this point was only the henhouse. Saying nothing, Lila walked around to the other side of the truck and opened the driver's side door and stepped back. Brad, a cautious cameraman, called Jill back down and said it was time to go and they would have their boss call to set up a proper interview. Lila thought that was a very good idea.

Lila sat down to make a few notes on how she would handle such an interview and decide whether she should let them take photographs of the shack, provided that there are no photos of the house or other outbuildings and no mention of the address or photos of the mailbox in front. And there were probably other issues she had not thought about. She called Vinnie and asked him to drop in when he had time as she wanted to run this by him to see how he felt about being interviewed and whether he thought she should allow them to photograph the shack. His presence there would hold the reporters at bay. Curt and a little frosty, Vinnie said that he might be able to drop in one night this week after work, but he was very busy. She tried to make small talk, but he cut her short, saying that he had an incoming call.

Lila showered and chose her best professional dress for her trip over to the university. Once again, she thought she really needed to update her doughty wardrobe. She was scheduled to meet with Professor Dumas who was mentioned in the alumni news as a key person involved in starting up educational retreats. Over the phone, he seemed interested in what Lila had to present as she gave him a brief description of the Swanson property and general location but that the owner had not yet decided how or when she wanted to make plans for future allocation of her estate. This was just a fact-finding mission on the owner's behalf, and no, Mrs. Swanson would not be coming with her for this initial interview but she did give her approval of the meeting. Making the most of the trip, Lila also planned to stop into the biochemistry department just for old times' sake. It had been years since her last visit.

Driving through the small village of Rockton, she noticed some flashing lights and a police car down the street where the new addition to the library was being constructed. As she slowed, she saw the Alma ambulance pulling out with flashing lights and sirens singing. She hoped it wasn't a serious construction accident. She had read in the *Alma Daily* that the Gabril Construction Company was in some sort of litigation with a former employee injured on another jobsite. Well, she would probably get all the scoop and more down at Jed's Café tomorrow morning. She hoped that Marguerite would be expecting her since she was quite enjoying pulling Marguerite into conversation while preparing the day's vegetables. It was beginning to feel like a symphony of quiet words, accommodating glances, and peeling motions, with each understanding the part that they played.

Professor Dumas was quite an affable man with an outgoing personality, small in stature but not lacking confidence. And a well-groomed goatee and sideburns added to his charm. In the beginning, Lila did not know how to initiate the conversation, but he eased her into it by asking about her background. She said that it was a far stretch for her, a biochemist, to take such an interest in a liberal arts project but recent events stirred her into seeing possibilities that she never knew existed before. Also the article about the Liberal Arts Educational Retreat in her alumni magazine and that the university was looking at various sites made her wonder if Goshen might not be a good fit. Lila said that if the retreat was eventually placed where she was suggesting, then he might want to call it Goshen Valley Retreat.

Now Professor Dumas was quietly encouraging her on with a slight nod and interested eyes, so she launched into the description of Goshen and the surrounding area. He asked her about the number of residences there now, and she said approximately five fully occupied and all five were quite some distance apart on large acreages as some had been peaches and apple orchards. Since she had used the term *fully occupied*, he asked her how many unoccupied residences might be there. She mentioned that there was one historically significant abandoned farm which had been built by the first homesteader back in the 1800s. When he seemed to be interested in the background of this historic farm, she hurried on to say that there was a horse rancher interested in restoring it and moving her riding academy there. A local builder did check it out and found it sound enough for such a project. However, holding the prime location in the Goshen area, with a sweeping view, was the estate she had come to talk about—the Swanson Manor—that could become the anchor for the retreat project.

Describing the Swanson Manor, she could go into quite a bit of detail which was still fresh in her mind. She started with the grand entry and the chandelier with the crystal teardrop pendants which twinkled with the sunlight and breeze. And from there, she moved into the front reception parlor where Howard and Genevieve's portraits still held court, overseeing all events. From there, she moved into the music parlor and told him about the grand piano and added a few childhood escapades of her own when the local children peeked into the windows. Realizing that she was adding too many flourishes, she decided to calm down and let him take the lead once again.

Professor Dumas allowed that this did sound interesting and asked how many rooms in all. Lila was not sure because she had not been invited to see the upstairs, but from hearsay, she thought there were six bedrooms upstairs and five rooms on the first floor and a maid's quarters added onto the back. She told him that it was built with the best of material in the early 1900s by a lumber baron, and her father said that there was a lot of black oak used in the construction. And the library was probably one of the finest that could be found in a modest community anywhere.

To this, he raised his interested eyebrows into arched arrows. Next he wanted to know if there were motel accommodations in the area for larger group meetings and concerts, etc. Lila admitted that they would have to travel to Alma for motel and hotel lodging since nearby village of Rockton had only a bed-and-breakfast accommodation of three rooms. But it occurred to her that some of the owners of the farmhouses in Goshen may see the potential of offering rooms and breakfast if they saw the opportunity.

Now showing moderate enthusiasm, he asked what she thought was the real asset of the community and how would it serve as a retreat for those interested in art, music, drama, and literature. Getting ready for this meeting, she had given this some thought; she was prepared to tell him about the rolling hills, the brooks and streams that find their way to the Susquehanna, the soft sweet drinking water and numerous stands of sugar maple and back oak trees. Also one can be rewarded with one of the finest views around if you are willing to pack binoculars and water and hike up to Caleb's Lookout on Crescent Ridge; from there, you can see forever. And the Stanton family left a colorful legacy of homespun, toe-tapping musical festivals. Niles and Nyla Stanton were the original homesteaders and built the farm that is now vacant. Their great-great-great-grandson is now very involved with the music industry in Nashville. Lila said she could take hours regaling him with Stanton stories but knew he did not have that kind of time.

Looking at his watch, he said, "Yes, I do have a class in fifteen minutes, but if you could come back in an hour and fifteen, we could go for a coffee and chat a little further."

"Okay, I had planned to check into the biochemistry department to talk to Dr. Fessenden, so I could come back then."

"Good," he responded, "I want to hear a little more about this Mrs. Swanson and see what you think her plans might be."

Lila was disappointed to learn that several of the professors she had hope to see, especially Dr. Fessenden who published extensively about alternative medicine, were away on vacation. However, she was lucky to bump into an organic chemistry professor, Dr. Langlau, who tried to fail her because she refused to come to lab when they were distilling the saturated fatty acid C-14, commonly known as myristic acid. Some fatty acids, such as C-14 ($C_{14}H_{28}O_2$), when separated from the other companion fats emit an extreme rank odor, and when this purified fatty acid wafted across Lila's sensitive nose, she became quite nauseous. They got into quite a tussle and Lila had to get a medical doctor's permit so she did not have to attend that particular lab procedure.

Now twenty-five years and hundreds of students later, she was shocked that he would remember her and the incident. They had quite a chuckle, reminiscing about how each remembered the story. Likely they both embellished the story in the retelling over the years. But the lab incident solved a little childhood mystery for Lila; she had to hold her nose when she drank whole milk and her brother did not. And she liked the taste of butter when baked or cooked but not raw. It still never ceased to amaze her that it was just a difference in the number of hydrogens stuffed into the saturated fatty acids that created the problem. So when the dairy industry started to package fat-free milk rather than feed it to the pigs, she was happy about this good fortune but worried a little for the pigs. Her father always told her that pigs were smarter than dogs and he had a story to prove it, so to speak.

Professor Dumas said that they could get a good cup of coffee at the student union, and it was a pleasant ten-minute walk; Lila was glad that she put on her sensible doughty shoes that morning. Settled in with their coffee and croissants, they exchanged small talk and gossip about the chemistry department. Professor Dumas asked Lila to call him by Theodore. Lila thought, *Hmmm, making progress. Soon it will be Ted or Teddy.*

Now they quickly segued into the discussion of Mrs. Swanson and he wanted to know a little of her background. Lila ran down the particulars and that there were probably no living relatives to whom she could or would bequeath the property. Here he cautioned that sometimes a long-lost relative, bubbles to the surface when there are resources underground: gas, coal, oil, water, or timber above ground. Lila discovered that Theodore liked to cut to the quick as he shortened Mrs. Swanson's name to the Swan and was now calling it The Swan Retreat. Lila was wondering how Mrs. Swanson would feel about that, but she thought that Professor Dumas could charm her into adopting the diminutive. *If Violet were here with me, she would turn on her beguiling smile and Teddy would meet his match.*

At this point, Professor Dumas showed his hand by revealing that he had done some research on the Swanson property before Lila's visit. He knew that the sixty-five acres attached to this property was only a small portion of the acreage which Mrs. Swanson owned because she was heir to another thousand acres in the county. This seemed logical because Lila recalled that her father had told her the tale of Howard Swanson's father and his ability to secure many acres in the township for timbering. And wisely, Theodore checked out the Department of Highways and found that they were exploring several possibilities for routing a new East-West expressway across the state and one of the possible routes came close to Goshen and the property in question. In ease of access, this might be a good thing; but if it were too close, it would be a noisy distraction. *Uh-oh*, thought Lila.

Walking back to Professor Dumas' office, they decided on a course of action. Theodore would continue to vet other sites and possibilities that have come to his attention. One such site was on a large dam with vacation homes nearby, but it had several drawbacks, one in particular, not much room to expand. Lila would continue to visit with Mrs. Swanson and establish how serious she might be. If she did show further interest, then Lila would encourage her to arrange a meeting with her lawyers to discuss the various ways that the donation could be accomplished and possibly then, a meeting with her tax accountants. Lila was beginning to feel a little optimistic with this developing passion for community service. Or was it just a response to the impending midlife crisis that would be coming on like a hot coal stove? She wished she could sit down with Violet and have a heart-to-heart.

When she drove in, Benny, anxious to prove that he was no slacker, came running out of his guard doghouse. Lila chuckled to see how serious he was. Of course, he was no Xavier and would not scare many; but at least, he would make a thief's job more difficult. Still in her go-to meeting clothes, they went immediately to call the hens in for the night and check the garden. The beans were healthy, and the kohlrabi was starting to show promise, and she might be able to pick sugar snap peas by next week. But she would need to water and weed tomorrow. She noticed that the Astrakhan apple tree was setting up small green apples already; the bees had done their job well last spring. This made her think that she should have told Theodore about the apple orchard above Mrs. Swanson's house. Possibly it could be restored to healthy condition with proper care and pruning. She remembered many the time that she and Violet roamed that orchard and had their fill of windfalls which they reasoned wasn't really stealing since they were not climbing up to harvest them. Well, maybe they did, just once or twice.

Checking her watch, she decided that this would be a good time to call Vinnie about the interview. But just then, Violet called and said that she was feeling the need to chat. Her treatments were going well. She wondered if everything was okay with Lila. This gave Lila the clue that it was a good time to talk about herself and share some local stories. They laughed about Mrs. Swanson's nickname, the Swan. And Lila thought it elegant, "And why had we not thought of that?"

Violet countered that she hoped that this was not Mrs. Swanson's swan song. "Well, that makes me swan," countered Lila.

Early next morning, an executive from Alma News called and asked Lila to come in for an interview tomorrow, but Lila thought Saturday afternoon would be better fit for Vinnie, the guy who helped her bring Buddy down from the shack. No, he was sorry but no studio appointments on Saturday, but of course, they could come out to film at her house.

"Exactly what I am trying to avoid. I will try to convince Vinnie to leave work early tomorrow as he is working over that way. We could be there by 4:30 p.m. I will call to let you know if that suits him. Of course, you understand that he will be in his construction clothes at that time of the day."

Immediately she called Vinnie. He sounded irritated and said that he might make it there by 4:30 p.m., "But go ahead and start because you never know with construction how or when the day would end."

A little exasperated, she called Alma News and confirmed the appointment for tomorrow afternoon, Vinnie or no, just get it done. After hanging up, she felt sure that Vinnie would not be there to help. It was becoming obvious that he felt rebuked and was holding her at arm's length.

Looking around in her spare kitchen, Lila decided to go to Jed's Café for coffee cake before meeting with Marguerite. Jed made the best zucchini nut bread which he served with a dab of whipped cream cheese, sweetened with honey. Besides if she went early, she would probably hear the town gossip about the ambulance coming out of the library parking lot yesterday, still hoping that it wasn't a construction accident. She went in and could tell the gossip was already in high gear as she pushed forward to sit up at the counter. The efficient waitress with the ponytail brought her a cup of coffee, with cream, before she even asked and motioned over to the pies and cakes. Yes, Lila would have a slice of zucchini bread. She listened while she had her little breakfast.

"Sad news about Johnnie, wasn't it? Too bad his sister didn't come for him last night. Someone should have called her. It was cold last night. Yvonne found him unconscious—slumped by the backdoor."

"But he is being kept alive in ICU, isn't he?"

"No, I heard warm blankets for hypothermia."

"Well, maybe they can get him into the bathtub. Heaven knows his sister can't! Although he might die of fright, if they try. Perhaps they should have tried before they woke him up."

"Maybe the hospital will get him into fresh clothes."

"Don't count on it, Good Samaritan has tried many times, but Johnnie says they are not 'comfible' and they smell funny."

"Well, it does not look good to have him sitting around on the doorsteps of our businesses, begging."

"That's not true, Rachel, he never begs. People just hand him a sandwich or a bag of chips when they leave the store. All the do-gooders around here are creating this problem. Someone should talk to his sister."

Since this conversation was winding down, Lila poured a cup of coffee for Marguerite and headed on back to the prep room. Marguerite was already busy and had half of the vegetables washed, peeled, or chopped. She said she heard them talking about Johnnie and said that she felt sorry for his sister. Johnnie has many complicated learning problems and he gets very agitated being held at home all day long. That is why she brings him in the morning and picks him up at night. On the doorsteps, here in Rockton, he can at least give a hello and a God bless occasionally.

Lila was most anxious to get Marguerite's assessment on the distillation process, but she decided to wait until Mar was willing to reveal her thoughts on the matter. Instead she related several amusing stories about Benny which brought a little smile from Marguerite, plus one of her own Xavier stories. It seemed that Marguerite's neighbors down the road apiece were trying to get rid of some skunks that had burrowed under the front porch. They were told by a friend that they should spray feminine douche of a particular brand on old socks and stuff them into the hole to flush them out. It was true that the skunks did not care for the douche-scented socks stuffed into their home. Rather than give up their cozy abode, they pitched out the foul socks, and by morning, the socks went missing and the skunks held fast.

Well, for three days running, the socks ended up on Marguerite's front doorstep. Since she routinely left Xavier out for his late-night run around ten o'clock, she decided to turn on the light to watch for him as he came back up the driveway; and sure enough, he had a sock in his mouth which he carefully placed on her front doorstep before coming to the side door for entry into the house. Chuckling, Marguerite said he was bringing her a "scented" present. Lila said it was good that he liked the scent of douche better than the scent of skunk.

Marguerite was an introverted person by nature, comfortable with her own thoughts, and never felt the need to fill the void with useless conversation. Therefore, Lila realized that she would have to broach the subject about her new lab equipment and were there any problems that she might be able to solve? Marguerite said no, everything was working well. She just needed more time to assess the results of the first distillation process since the products that she was obtaining were not identical to the old alembic method.

Lila guessed that this would happen but said perhaps she could get some help with identifying products; she still had access to the labs over in Brookfield. This would come with its own complications, however, since the supervisor would have the right to know what she was analyzing. Marguerite had a great deal of pride in her work and would not be keen to hand over her proprietor products. *Perfectly understandable*, thought Lila. Of course, now the problem will be how to tell Jed why the process was taking such a long time. Understandably he was anxious to have the elixir for his grandson.

On the other hand, one of the first things she might offer Marguerite was a keen sense of smell and taste. Lila was thinking back to high school and college chemical analyses quizzes where she could identify some unknowns just by taking a sniff. She went through the normal stepwise procedures, just to see if she was right and, of course, to get a good grade. Besides if you liked your lab partner (his last name also stated with a W), the experiments were fun. All this aside, Lila sensed that she would have to wait for Marguerite's invitation. For an alchemist, there is a normal pace and rhythm to life that requires patience.

Lila stopped in at the local library to visit with Yvonne who was quite energized by the construction of the new wing being added to her tiny library. Yvonne had been the librarian forever, and here, she ruled supreme; and she would die a happy woman knowing that she had made a truly worthwhile contribution to her little town. This made Lila think about Mrs. Swanson's possible donation of her estate for the Swan Retreat over in Goshen, but it was too soon to share that info with anyone. Lila asked Yvonne if she had found any more information on giant hogweed.

Smiling, Yvonne handed her a small brochure put out by the state, saying that it was illegal to sell, purchase, or plant giant hogweed due to its toxic nature. Unfortunately it did not mention how to identify the differences between the less toxic cousins such as cow parsnips. They should have consulted Mrs. Swanson's library before publishing this scary brochure. In retrospect, Lila wished that she had visited the botany department at the university instead of biochemistry. Perhaps next time. Yvonne wanted to know if Lila knew how Johnnie was progressing, but Lila only knew what gossip was being traded at Jed's Café. "And you know how reliable that is."

Wanting a new hairstyle for the TV interview, Lila stopped at Shear Beauty to make an appointment for tomorrow morning. Once again, she would have to wear one of her outdated go-to meeting dresses, but there was no time for shopping right now. And anyway, who cares what the bee lady wears? She remembered Hildegarde, from grade school, wearing only the latest fashions. I should try to find Hildegarde and see if she went into fashion design, a perfect career choice for her.

Back home and over a very late lunch and a glass of iced tea, she thought about tomorrow's schedule. After her hair appointment, she would stop at Mrs. Swanson's in the late morning before lunch and explain what she found out from Professor Dumas and his recommendations. She decided to phone an old chum, Shirley, now a lawyer with Barclay and Barclay in Alma, to set up an appointment for early afternoon. Who knows, there might be a little time left over for shopping.

While she was deep in thought about tomorrow, Adeeb called to ask if he could come over to Rockton this weekend. He said he needed to get away for a small road trip and it might be fun to see Lilaland. And in addition, he wanted to bring his latest data for her to see. When she asked if there was a problem, he said he wasn't sure but needed to discuss this with her. He already cleared the trip with his supervisor who agreed to supplement Lila's small allowance.

Looking up at her calendar, she noticed that she had tentatively scheduled Caroline in for Saturday to start her garden irrigation project, but that could be rescheduled. She agreed that he could come and she would set up accommodations at the local B and B which had a reputation as homey and comfortable but no frills. Since, he said, batching alone without his wife here, he was not used to the frills anymore. But he would like to take her out to dinner on Saturday night, if that was okay with her.

The following day, Lila was getting a little nervous so she arrived a little early at Shear Beauty. Bernice smiled and allowed that she could take her right in, and she had that look that said anything will be an improvement. After shampooing, cutting, setting, and blow drying, Lila finally peeked in the mirror, then took a second, and then a third peek, and thought to herself, *With this new hairdo, I look younger and sort of pretty in a Lila sort of way.*

Bernice smiled and said, "You should come in more often, you know."

"Yes, I can see that you do perform miracles."

She left Bernice smiling with a handsome tip. She checked again in the car mirror to make sure that she was right about the sort-of-pretty.

Mrs. Swanson was dismayed that Benny wasn't tagging along, and she expressed surprise about Lila's new hairdo. "My gosh, if it were any day but Wednesday, I might not have known you."

Lila was delighted with her response as she swirled her new hairdo for effect. "Come in for a spot of tea and tell me your latest news about Violet."

Lila related that Violet was doing okay with her first treatments but she had a long road ahead of her. She gave her Violet's address and said that she was sure that she would appreciate cards and notes. Finally she related her conversations with Professor Dumas concerning a retreat in Goshen. He had other sites under consideration, but he believed that it would be helpful if Mrs. Swanson would start conversations with her lawyer on possible avenues for estate donations.

Lila bravely charged ahead and asked, "Would it be okay for me to set up an appointment with Shirley at Barclay and Barclay?"

Mrs. Swanson thought that would be okay since she was not completely satisfied with her last experience with Smith, Smith & Jackson. Lila coyly asked if SS&J handled the library donation.

"Yes, that was the case, how did you know?" she asked.

Lila said that it was just a good guess. They both chuckled. And Lila was secretly chuckling about Theodore's nickname for Mrs. Swanson.

At the law office of Barclay and Barclay, Shirley advised her to insist that Alma News not give out her address and advised her how to handle the situation. Lila related to Shirley that soon, Mrs. Swanson may need some legal advice about options for bequeathing some of her property. Yes, Shirley understood that Mrs. Swanson had donated a large sum of money to the little Rockton library. Lila did not let on that this was the second confirmation on the identity of the donor, but she was thinking, *Pretty good deduction on my part?* Lila asked Shirley if she would be willing to sit down with Mrs. Swanson and herself a week from today, just for an introductory session. Mornings would be best as Mrs. Swanson naps in the afternoon.

With time left before the 4:30-interview, Lila found Clair's boutique on the side street that had some interesting fashions in the window; those targeted for mature women instead of teenagers. She found several that suited her but decided on only one since her opportunity for dress up was limited. While still wearing the outfit of choice, she asked them to cut the tags off and she walked out of the boutique a brand-new woman. Brimming with confidence, she drove over to Alma News and entered fifteen minutes early and asked to talk with the producer who had set up the appointment, and he agreed with her privacy issues. She sat down near a window to wait and watch for Vinnie.

The interview went well, brief and professional, but no sign of Vinnie whose presence would have thawed Jill's frosty composure and loosened her girdle a notch. "Well, so much for the eighteen-dollar-haircut, plus four-dollar-tip and the forty-dollar-outfit. Best to put it all behind me. I was not cut out to be a celebrity anyway."

Jill caught up to Lila just as she was leaving and she said that they would find another way to get up to Buddy's shack. She knew that the more-friendly neighbors would allow them up through their property. After all, it was not on Lila's property. "Whose property do you think it is?" Lila asked.

Jill said, "A quick check at town hall would reveal ownership."

With an amused smile, Lila said, "Yes, I can assure you that it does."

Imagining an impending scene between Jewel and Jill, Lila almost burst into an out-loud laugh.

On the drive home, she thought about the interview and what she should have said when Jill insinuated that she should have pulled all the pieces together when she first noticed the missing items in the bee barn. Lila always thought of clever responses later after she had a chance to mull over the conversation. Or had a chance to sleep on it. She wasn't sure she wanted to watch herself on the six o'clock news. She was now regretting that she had agreed to this folly anyway.

When she got out of the car, Benny came running but stopped short and awkwardly stared at this new phenomenon. He was a lot happier when she changed into her barn clothes to attend the chores. Even Benny did not think much of this attempt at stardom. That evening, Lila half-expected Vinnie to call with his excuses, but no call came.

In retrospect, good things did happen today; the impending meeting with the lawyer and Mrs. Swanson next week was real progress. And she was happy that she and Mrs. Swanson were continuing the intimate relationship that had its germinal seed planted when Violet visited. She called Caroline to change the scheduled Saturday irrigation project and arranged for a Friday-morning-planning meeting. Tomorrow, after her visit with Marguerite at Jed's, she would touch up the bee barn a little bit for Adeeb's visit this weekend and set up his reservation at Rosella's B and B. While planning for lunch snacks and drinks, she started to wonder how you could entertain someone here in Rockton who had lived for years in London. Since it was too preposterous to even consider, it made her tone down her expectations. She did not have a museum exhibiting royal jewels, but she did have six queens up in the bee barn, each in command of their own monarchy.

Finally Lila did take her sandwich into the living room to watch the news, and when her five-minute claim to fame was aired, she was pleasantly surprised to see that she did not look as ill at ease as she had felt and instead, it was Jill who looked a little scattered and a little too eager to steal the spotlight. And besides, that short hemline exposed unattractive legs. Someone in wardrobe at Alma News needs to advise the young things. Just because the hemlines have risen above the knee, not everyone should buy into the New York and Paris fashion guru edicts. "But then, maybe I am being unkind to a sister trying to make her way in a competitive business. And someone with a barn-coat wardrobe shouldn't throw pitchforks."

The next morning, Samuel came peddling up the driveway, and after searching around a bit, he found Lila up at the henhouse. He took over the feed sack and replenished the feeders and softly clucked to the hens in a manner of a boy quite used to farm chores. Watching him at such ease in this setting, she remembered to ask him about Albert and Dixie, the now-famous llama-and-pig couple. Samuel thought all was well as long as they could sleep together in their own special pen. His father thought this was unseemly and wanted to separate the two, but after several nights of Albert squalling and Dixie snorting, he decided to allow the cohabitation after all. Smiling Lila thought of her lovely neighbors, Jewel and Jack, who seemed about as unlikely a couple as Albert and Dixie.

Noticing Samuel's new growth and strength, Lila asked if he thought he might like to work for her now and then when she had trips out of town or when she needed a lift from time to time. He said that he would have to ask his parents, but he was willing if they could spare him from his own farm chores. "Perhaps I could stop and talk to your mom one day soon and inquire."

Samuel thought that would be best. From there, they moved on up to the bee barn where Lila had to bring some beehive frames down from the overhead loft. She had removed some filled honey frames from the hives last week, and she needed to replace those with new ones as the summer flowers would blossom soon.

As she was handing the frames down to Samuel, he looked around rather skeptically and said that she needed to install a pulley system like he and his father had done for moving heavy loads down from their barn loft. He went on to describe the rope-and-pulley system that they used. This made a lot of sense since Lila remembered the pulley system on the hayfork in the Stanton barn. Finally when getting ready to leave, Samuel pulled a few rumpled dollars from his pocket and said that his mother had sent him down for a large jar of honey. "Well, Samuel, please tell your mother that you earned this jar of honey. No further payment is necessary."

After showering and looking at the time, she realized that she had missed prep time with Marguerite but knew that she could catch up with her next week. The processes in her laboratory dictated their own time clock and season, adhering to principles set down ages ago by folks who had the wisdom of patience. She stopped at Jed's Café with his egg order, and yes, Marguerite had already gone home. This gave her a chance to swing by the hardware and feed store to purchase rope and pulleys, plus chicken feed. Once back home, she spent all afternoon tidying around the house and up at the bee barn to get ready for Adeeb's visit. She did not want to think that she was trying to impress him, but then again, maybe she was; however, it was quite unlikely that she could impress someone who came from a privileged background of servants and helpmates. She pulled out her recipe files to decide what to serve for lunches—tomorrow for Caroline and later for Adeeb's visit.

Dear Violet,

As I sit here tonight, by a comforting tiny log fire, I am thinking of you and wondering if your treatments are progressing on schedule. Have they given you anything for nausea? I wish I could be there for support and brew a nice pot of tea. I am wondering if a visit would be welcome after you get through this first set of treatments. I could plan for the management of the henhouse and Benny's care, and the bees take care of themselves as long as they have enough wax foundation in their frames. Perhaps we could take a side trip over to the Grove Park Inn in Ashville. I hear that lunch on the terrace is exceptional.

All is progressing with Mrs. Swanson. As I told you, I made the initial trip over to the university to meet with Professor Dumas about the retreat. They have several properties in mind, but I think we can persuade him to move Goshen to the top of the list. Mrs. Swanson and I will meet with Shirley next week, just for a preliminary discussion about bequeathing property. Shirley remembered you and passed along hellos and good wishes.

Caroline is still very interested in purchasing your homestead, and I must arrange a meeting with Vinnie. I will have them all for a cookout soon. But here is the amazing thing—I saw a large handsome table in her kitchen the other day when I stopped by to talk about her irrigation system for her horses. She did not say anything when I commented, but I am almost sure it was your family table, around which we used to wolf down some of Holly's buttery pancakes, dripping with raspberry syrup. It was completely restored and had a different color, but it sure sat the same. So that is another thing Caroline could bring back to the farm restoration, along with the Victrola and the birds-eye maple bedroom furniture. We are getting closer to complete, if only we could find the missing commode.

Finally did you know that Vinnie was not divorced? Only thinking about it! I imagine that one day, he and his wife will reconcile. I hear that she is also dating but does not have a serious relationship.

I am always thinking of you and sending good wishes, but the prevailing winds are against me since they pass over Tennessee first before reaching Pennsylvania. On the other hand, it is comforting to think that some of those breezy particles might be bringing me a message from Gatlinburg.

Love always,
Lila

Caroline arrived in the morning after breakfast, but she said she had time for a quick cup of coffee while joking that she did not know how to react around a TV celebrity, making Lila laugh. On a slower day, she hoped they could hike up to the shack. "I remember when we used to swim up in the strippings, but I don't remember the shack."

Caroline had already had breakfast, fed the horses, mucked out the stalls, and repaired a bridle. A one-woman dynamo. They started out at Lila's garden to plan the irrigation route down from Alder Run, calculated the kind and amount of tubing needed, along with various connections and filters. Lila had to purchase the supplies before their next meeting. Caroline was all business today which left no time for visiting, but she was willing to come to a cookout next week; most evenings were free, so they could plan around Vinnie's schedule. Caroline checked out Benny's quill punctures and was pleased with his progress.

Adeeb arrived midafternoon, dressed in comfy casual, carrying a bouquet of flowers and sporting a million-dollar smile. Such attention made Lila a little flustered, but he immediately put her at ease, looking for a container to arrange the flowers. She pointed him to the sideboard in the dining room which had an assortment of containers. After taking in the cottage decor, he chose an antique metal flute with a handle that received the arrangement perfectly. Lila set up a small welcoming lunch out on the patio, and Adeeb brought the flowers to the outdoor table. Benny cautiously circled around the patio several times, not sure of his own status here. Was this some competition for Lila's affection or just a quick howdy-do? Finally Adeeb made several gestures that people must use in Pakistan and Benny came to him and sat down like a prince to be petted. Benny must understand Pakistani.

Anxiously Adeeb wanted a little tour of Lilaland before they sat down for serious scientific discussions. He brought in a small handsome leather briefcase, reminding himself that they had things to discuss, but he surreptitiously slid it out of sight so that they could relax for a moment before getting down to work. But Lila convinced him that it would be best to check in at the B and B first, and afterward, they could take a ten-minute walking tour of Rockton.

Adeeb joked that he thought he might have seen all of Rockton on his way here. Lila went along to make the introductions at the B and B. Rosella took him off, arm in arm, to prove that her accommodations were the best in Rockton, albeit the only accommodation for miles around. Lila heard a lot of clucking and "Oh my" from where she waited, back in the reception area. She could tell Rosella was winning him over with all the little touches she had added to her old homestead, including a sitting porch which wrapped around two sides of the house. She gave him the room with the view, looking over her prize-winning flower garden. She described a full breakfast for the morning and he should just let her know if he forgot anything that he might need. She gave him a key and said that she liked for all guests to be in by midnight. Lila was thinking, *How quaint*, but then, except for Buster's clientele on Friday night, everyone was home by midnight.

Sensing that Adeeb still wanted to stretch his legs a bit before opening that briefcase, Lila asked if he wanted to meet her animal menagerie before they tackled the serious stuff.

"Perfect, I was hoping that I could."

She wondered if he brought any barn shoes since he would not want to wear that expensive pair of Italian loafers up to a chicken yard. Well, yes, at the last minute, he did throw a pair of hiking boots into the car. Since chickens are not sophisticated animals with private toilets, Lila sensed disaster, but he was still smiling after he snugged on his hiking boots. He stood there, stomping around a bit, posing for her and making a little fun of himself. Frankly in those boots, along with his comfy casual attire, he looked like one of those models in the *LL Bean* catalog, making Lila smile to herself.

They walked and talked, and Adeeb asked a lot of chicken-and-egg questions. Lila was wondering if he was going to ask the proverbial question, but no, he did not. From a high perch, George looked down on Adeeb quite suspiciously, switching his head from side to side as though the eye on the other side of his head could better decipher what he was seeing. Briefly Lila touched on the fact that she just lost beautiful Henrietta and Brigitte was now at the top of the pecking order, but that was a long story for another time. He smiled (oh, that smile again) and said he had until Sunday. Still smiling, Adeeb allowed that perhaps George thought Brigitte was beautiful.

They walked over to the garden and checked out the vegetables; he was impressed with the beautiful kale plants. She pulled a couple of sugar snap peas for snacking as they hiked up to the bee barn. He apparently had some exposure to an apiary as a young lad, so he did not ask many beekeeping questions, but he was quite intent on studying the setup. Enjoying the quiet moment, they sat down and watched the orderly exiting-and-entering language, the sun dance messages being passed, and guard bees keeping strict order. For a while, they sat in silence, content to just watch seventy thousand bees (times six) going about their business. He observed that the political leaders should sit here for a day before trying to solve the world problems. Lila was thinking that a hike up to Caleb's might be an even better problem solver.

The afternoon was slipping away, they decided to cut the sightseeing tour short and head back to the cottage and the briefcase. Lila was getting a stipend for her consulting service and she felt the need to be responsible for time spent. Adeeb agreed that it was probably a good idea. They had a lot of territory to cover and he thought she would be surprised with his findings.

"Pleasant surprises?" she asked.

"We shall see," he replied. They ambled back down to the cottage, somewhat reluctantly, with Lila a little apprehensive of what the data might reveal. She invited him to spread out his data on the dining room table since she had only a tiny office which was once the pantry. Lila was anxious to see the results of the collagen fractionation, but Adeeb wanted to start with his results on the isolation and identification of autoantibodies from lupus patients so she agreed that they could start there. Adeeb had made great progress identifying subsets of autoimmune responses in seventy-eight patients studied. They went over the data with a microscopic view, and Lila described a new immunofluorescent test she had heard about from a friend at NIH.

After several hours of intense give-and-take, Lila asked if he liked pizza and he said that he learned to like it after several months in this country. Each decorated half of a pizza with their choice of toppings. While the pizza was cooking, they sat out on the patio with a beer, another thing that he had to learn to like but he had acquired that taste at several famous London pubs. He said that he did miss London's historic pubs; his favorite was the Lamb and Flag in Covent Garden, close to his apartment. In the 1800s, Charles Dickens spent many a night there with his literary buddies as the tale is told. Even if he spent only one night there, who could question the claim now? And it makes for good press, just like Hemingway hanging out at Les Deux Margots in Paris where the souls of poets hover about the diners. Adeeb allowed that what made the Lamb and Flag entertaining was the Dickens quote game. After several strong ales, everyone tried to quote Dickens—badly—in order to get the best vote. The funnier the misquote, the bigger the vote. The one with the most votes received a drink on the house. He said that assured that Dickens was read and reread, conniving a misquote or two.

What a culture shock to end up in Brookfield, Lila ventured. Guessing where this thinking was headed, he said that for the moment, Brookfield was what he needed for his career—less pubs and more science. Just as she entered the house to check the pizza, she heard a truck pull into the driveway but she needed to get the pizza out before it overcooked. When she came out, Adeeb said that someone, in a construction van, pulled into the driveway but he must have had the wrong address as he turned around and left.

After dinner, they spent an hour on the collagen research. He said he made a startling discovery of several new components that revealed themselves when he used the low pH buffer, the one which may have been tampered with by someone. After he locked down his lab and had his lab tech carefully titrate the buffer back up to standard, the new components disappeared. They ran the procedure again, this time, with the pH of the tampered buffer, and voila, there they were; so unwittingly, whoever tried to sabotage his work actually catapulted him months ahead. He was not sure who had tampered with the buffers, but he noticed that Harold was quite disdainful about the locked doors, saying that Adeeb was destroying the culture of trust enjoyed at Brookfield.

By now, both were starting to yawn so she walked him out to his car and agreed that he should return tomorrow after breakfast. She had the feeling that Rosella would be hurt if he did not stay for her breakfast strata; she was obviously proud of her cooking skills. Lila had heard from others that they were top-notch. Better get your money's worth, as they say here in Rockton. In parting, he reminded Lila that he wanted to take her out to dinner tomorrow night.

"Yes," she said, "I made reservations at Michael's, our only restaurant in Rockton. I hope that is okay."

Lila woke up to George's good morning doodle-doo and decided that after chores, she would hurry down to Jed's Café. Adeeb mentioned that he would like to meet Marguerite since he had studied Ayurveda medicine while in Pakistan. Lila had no way to contact Marguerite on the weekend, but she wondered if Jed might have a contact. Also she remembered that she had seen wires strung on poles when she drove up Possum Crossing, but that may have only been for electric service.

As she entered the café, Burt called out, "Well, if it isn't our queen bee celebrity joining us today. I hear she has started a detective service for finding lost individuals."

Sonny said she should call it The Bees-Knees. Another voice called out, "That is none of your beeswax."

Now Lila remembered why she did not usually have breakfast here.

Sliding into the swivel stool, which had been recovered in red vinyl, Lila suddenly remembered that Sonny had relatives over in the East Valley and was actually related to Marguerite. Jed brought Lila a cup of coffee, and Lila gave Jed two dozen eggs and a jar of honey. No, Jed did not have a telephone number for Marguerite. He usually just drove over and waited until she secured Xavier. He suggested that she might do the same, but that might not make the best impression on her new friend. *Uh-oh*, thought Lila, *the grapevine travels fast in Rockton.*

She asked quietly, "How do her East Valley clients get in touch when they need medicinal treatments and tonics? Surely, they can't sit there in their cars, waiting for her to confine Xavier. That doesn't sound like good business practices."

Half-jokingly, Jed allowed that there was probably a secret code passed out to most of the residents in East Valley that Xavier understands.

Noticing an empty chair at Burt and Sonny's table, Lila picked up her coffee, walked over, and asked if she might have a word with Sonny. Of course, Rachel, several tables over, was trying hard not to notice and failing badly. Burt sat there, dumbstruck and mute for a few seconds. Gently Sonny got up and pulled out a chair.

"Sonny, I have a friend in town who would like to visit with Marguerite. He has some background in her field of alternative medicine. In fact, he studied with a practitioner for several years in Pakistan."

Lila sipped and watched Sonny's eyes over her coffee cup and waited for this info to take hold on his face. "And my friend is leaving tomorrow morning, so today is the only time I have to take him over to meet her. Does she have a telephone? I thought I saw telephone poles along Possum Crossing."

Sonny said that she did have a telephone but that was not the customary way of things; most of her clients in the East Valley had a Xavier code which they were not allowed to pass along to just anybody.

"I would like to give you the code but that would break her trust in me."

"With a prescient idea," Lila asked, "does it have to do with the number of times one blinks the car lights?"

Sonny folded his arms across his chest and feebly shook his head, sort of in the no direction.

"Well, never mind, I think it best to wait for another time when I can better prepare Marguerite for this meeting, so thanks anyway. Enjoyed having coffee with both of you."

Suddenly Burt found his lost voice, "Say, Lila, do bees have knees?"

"Well, yes, Burt, they do, but they do not have kneecaps."

"Well, I'll be a bee's uncle!"

Back home, just as Lila was explaining to Adeeb why they could not meet with Marguerite today, the phone rang. It was Sonny, saying that he talked with Marguerite and she said it was okay for Lila and her friend to come over around two o'clock. She was a little disappointed that it was not Violet, but he explained that it was someone with alternative medicine experience.

"I could not think of that big word you used to describe the practice, but I thought it started with an A and she knew right away what it was."

"Thanks, Sonny, I owe you a jar of honey."

With some time to spare, Lila and Adeeb walked up to Alder Run and sat on the bridge, listening to the trickling water running beneath them. Lila wanted to know a bit more about his Ayurveda background and what exactly does the word mean? Adeeb said that he attended a college while in Pakistan which had been started by a well-known practitioner from India. He moved his school there after the falling out between the two country's ideologies. From Sanskrit, the word translates to "science of life," but he personally thought a better translation of Ayurveda was "fullness of life." It is a holistic approach to wellness and the practice of healing which originated in India thousands of years ago. Through traditional techniques, it seeks to bring into balance the mind, body, and spirit. The major emphasis is to prevent illnesses by promoting good health practices from birth to old age. And this is done by a natural balance of cleansing, meditation, massage, herbal elixirs, vitamins, minerals, and a little yoga thrown into the mix as needed.

Lila noticed he did not mention water spa treatments, and she described an event several years ago, during a bad patch, when she scheduled a week in Saratoga at a lovely B and B where she had signed up for warm water baths and a massage to follow. After cooling down, she was put through several relaxing exercises where she had to clear the mind and practice several forms of breathing. She left her problems at home and roamed about Saratoga, enjoying much of the atmosphere, even went over to the track at 6:00 a.m., just to watch those beautiful horses on their morning workout which inspired her to visit the Racing Hall of Fame. She knew that this treatment set her straight for about a month, but then life got in the way and she did not continue with the faith.

Adeeb said that was normal and he did not have the answer for "backslippers."

"Backsliders, you mean." Together they laughed at his faux pas.

Lila asked Adeeb if he thought he might return to a practice which would combine both scientific and natural healing medicines. He thought that was possible since he did have his doctorate in both. Sitting there in disbelief, Lila calculated that this man had three doctorates, an MD, a PhD, and a doctor of Ayurveda. Dr.-Dr.-Dr. Guy! His wall of credits would be crowded with framed degrees. But for now, he said that he was happy to make his small contribution to research and immunotherapy.

Lila took Adeeb over into the meadow, just below the sugar maples, to search for teaberries. The time was right for their ripening and she could spot the small ground-hugging plant which, when searched, they found the tiny delicious red berry. Her mother and grandmother claimed that they had great power for promoting healthy metabolic possesses, but Lila only knew she loved the flavor.

After trying several, Adeeb agreed they were unusual and most delicious. He wondered how she described the flavor. And she said the only description was teaberry, just like the teaberry gum and teaberry ice cream. If they had the time, she would take him to the Alma Creamery to try the ice cream.

In the car, Lila was thinking, perhaps she should describe to Adeeb what they would find at Marguerite's, especially Xavier and his usual greeting at the car. But she decided to keep quiet and enjoy the ride through East Valley. Mar knew that they were scheduled, she would probably have Xavier already corralled inside. And Adeeb seemed to be content to take life as it comes, probably learned from his Ayurveda training. Who knows, he might even enjoy Xavier's inspection. And she knew he had dog language from watching him with Benny. Now she was getting curious how he might get on with Xavier.

As she pulled up Marguerite's driveway, Xavier's absence almost disappointed her. She turned off the engine and said they should wait just a few minutes just to make sure he was not out and about. When she rolled down the window, she could hear barking coming from inside the cabin. All safe, so they slowly walked up to the side door of the laboratory.

Mar stepped out to greet them, and, with her head tilted forty-five degrees, she used her special sideways look at this new friend. Lila made the introductions, and Adeeb gave a slight curtsy with his hands locked in a kind of greeting that many would call worship. This seemed to have some meaning to Mar as she peered straight up into his face which now was awash in a radiant smile. *Oh my gosh*, thought Lila, *that is the exact smile Violet had used to gain Mar's confidence.*

Smiling was not a habit in Lila's early years, so it did not come naturally to her. Violet always told her that she did not face smile, but she knew that her heart had. It was apparent that Adeeb also knew how to ease into a situation as he asked if they might see her gardens first. This seemed to have the same effect as three cups of tea back in Pakistan and was quicker.

After the garden inspection, they entered the laboratory. Lila held back, letting Adeeb have a moment to digest what he was about to see. She was not disappointed as he was clearly knocked off his pins to see this startling and beautiful collection of natural healing herbs and essential oils. Glancing back at Lila, his sparkling eyes spoke volumes. Marguerite was silent, but only for a moment, as they both rushed to talk about past experiences where they found many common interests and teachings. His grandfather knew such and such and her granddaddy knew him too.

"And did you know the great Austie?"

"No, but my father met him in Karachi."

Lila tucked herself away from the tornado and let the warm winds of conversation blow over her countenance while savoring the moment. On the way home, they were silent, both realizing that words would fail to describe what had just happened. She dropped him off at Rosella's B and B and he said he would pick her up at 6:30 p.m. for their dinner date at Michael's.

Since the visit at Marguerite's had taken longer than expected, Lila came home, rushing to get chores done and give Benny some much-needed attention. After a very short rest and shower, Lila rushed to get ready for her dinner engagement, still reluctant to call it a date. This was just a meeting, part of her commitment to Brookfield, after all. But still, she felt a tingle of excitement, knowing that Adeeb was enjoying her company, even though just as a female colleague. She knew, from Brookfield personnel records, that she was twelve years older than Dr. Guy.

Getting dressed, she was secretly happy that she had purchased that new outfit for her TV interview. The figure looking back at her from the full-length mirror said, "Not bad, girl, even Violet would approve." Watching from the bedroom alcove, Benny took a second look, even though he would have preferred her barn coat.

Adeeb arrived, dressed in an expensively tailored suit and some very polished dress shoes. Lila was wondering if this was not a bit excessive for Rockton, but it was always dimly lit on Saturday night at Michael's and no one will even notice. And anyway, she had asked for her favorite table, snugged privately over in the corner. What she had not anticipated was the long circuitous route needed to get to their table. Maybe Lila just imagined that every head turned in sequence as they passed by. Maybe Adeeb was not as handsome as Omar. Maybe she was being overly insecure tonight from inexperience in these situations.

As they sat down, Adeeb gave her a confident and reassuring smile and told her how lovely she looked. *My gosh*, she thought, *ever the gentleman*. She was wondering if he ever got aggravated and stomped around and acted like a peeved child. This thought made her relax a little.

While waiting for their drinks, Lila realized that even though she had her back to the room, she could see most of it in the mirror which was on the wall directly behind Adeeb. She was a little startled when she looked up and saw Vinnie. To her surprise, Vinnie and a date were only two tables behind her and it did not look like his wife. It looked to her as though Vinnie was stretching in order to better see who she was with, and in response, his date was nearly twisting out of her chair. Quickly Lila looked down and was determined not to glance at the mirror again.

Lila started conversation by asking about Adeeb's favorite London restaurants. It surprised her to learn that he preferred small, out-of-the-way places, not usually listed in Conde Nast, places that most people never took the time to find and those with an international menu.

"As you know, Great Britain has never been noted for great food. Also after long workdays, we often dined right at the pub."

Lila remembered that he preferred the Flag and Lamb. Chuckling, he corrected her, "The Lamb and Flag."

"Ah yes, where Dickens wiled away so many hours with his literary friends. David Copperfield was lucky to have ever been born. Whenever did he find the time to put pen to paper, let alone help Ms. Dickens give birth to ten little Dickens?"

Smiling, Adeeb said, "Perhaps someone else was helping him out at home."

This made Lila chuckle.

"In response to any bad turn of events, my mother used to say, 'Now isn't that a dickens of a note?' Or in surprise, she would ask, 'What the dickens?' It has just now dawned on me that these familiar phrases all emanated from his writing."

Adeeb allowed that Charles Dickens was indeed often quoted and humorously misquoted as they use to do at the Lamb and Flag.

To misquote Dickens, one of his pub buddies used to say that he had been so flummboxed by his wife that the devil now cared. Lila asked Adeeb if he ever wondered what might have been Tiny Tim's ailment. Yes, he often tried to guess what Dickens was alluding to, perhaps a nephrology issue, but it was difficult to judge medical conditions written about in the 1800s.

Over dinner, Adeeb decided to be very blunt and tell Lila that he was authorized by at least one supervisor at Brookfield to let her know that she was welcome anytime she wished to come back. He said that they had not fully appreciated her contribution until she was no longer there. But he was a little vague when she inquired about improved working conditions and would they address the reasons she decided to take this leave.

He was not sure about that, but he wanted to make one thing very clear. "You are needed at Brookfield, and I would very much like to have you as a collaborator."

Lila said that she was pretty satisfied with the little life she had carved out, but she would give it some thought. He lifted his wine glass, offering a little toast, and as Lila lifted hers in response, she glanced at the mirror and saw that Vinnie was looking directly back at her. He nodded and raised his glass. She gulped a sip and quickly put her head down, hoping Adeeb had not noticed.

Adeeb asked, "Friend of yours?" Lila admitted that he was an acquaintance. "Well, he sure has his date a little flummboxed."

To which Lila responded, "And now the devil does care."

Adeeb laughed. "You would have been stellar at the Lamb and Flag."

They decided to be very indulgent and share the decadent tiramisu, one plate, two forks. He slid his chair over beside Lila and gently put his arm on the back of her chair. Lila was afraid to look up in the mirror, but Adeeb said that they should at least give them something to talk about. His brown eyes were sparkling.

Lila said, "Now you are the devil, aren't you?"

It seemed that Adeeb was not through taunting the ogling couple. As Lila tried to put an inch of distance between them, Adeeb held her chair in place and whispered, "They won't know that we are just talking about some dry research or about the possibility that you will come back to the lab soon. Besides, wouldn't you like an after-dinner coffee? Rosella is not expecting me anytime soon."

Gently changing the focus of interest, Lila ask Adeeb when his wife was coming for a visit; she had heard that Arezo might be coming this summer and she would like to meet her. Since Arezo was now such a London girl, he was a little worried about how to entertain her. He planned for two days in the Big Apple, with dinner and a show, but wondered what to do after that. Lila said if she knew a little about Arezo, she could give him some ideas. He revealed that unlike his own background, she was originally from a small village north of Karachi. Generally she liked hiking. scaling tall peaks in the Himalayas, bicycling and exploring down country roads.

Pleasantly surprised, Lila said, "I like her already. The Alleghenies have no K2, not even a Mount Marcy, but there are some pleasant hikes with splendid views near here. A weekend trip to the Poconos might be a fun getaway, starting at the charming town of Mauch Chunk (Sleeping Bear), named by the Lenni Lanape Indians. The town decided that it no longer wanted to be a Sleepy Bear, so they changed the name to Jim Thorpe, in honor of a Pennsylvania's Olympic athlete. I personally prefer the heritage name of Mauch Chunk, but who can argue with success. While at the visitor center, you could learn about bicycle trails, white-water rafting, kayaking, tenting, and musical concerts. If thirsty, you could grab a brew at several lively pubs. And the Appalachian Trail runs close to this vicinity. Although I have been told that the trail is quite rocky in this part of Pennsylvania.

"Then from Brookfield, many New York venues are reachable in a one-day trip. Arezo might find Chautauqua interesting with the variety of venues they offer. Who knows, she may even enjoy a touristy trip to Niagara Falls and then a side trip to Niagara on the lake to the Shaw Festival."

"Would that be George Bernard Shaw?"

"Yes, they have made quite an institution there based on his many famous plays. Shaw is also very quotable. My favorite is, 'If you cannot get rid of the family skeleton, you may as well make him dance.'"

For a few minutes, they sparred with several Shaw misquotes and laughed about a few skeletons dancing in their own closets.

Adeeb checked his watch and Lila laughed. "You might be late for Rosella's curfew."

He signaled for the check and Lila finished her decaf. While in the middle of figuring out the tip, Adeeb looked up and said, half-jokingly, "It is sad that we did not meet a few years ago."

After a small hesitation, Lila countered, "I am finding that many things in life are lost but for want of better timing."

After paying the tab, Adeeb made several gentlemanly gestures, holding Lila's chair and gently guiding her through the restaurant with his hand lightly placed on her shoulder instead of the elbow. Knowing the game that he was playing and obviously enjoying, she was determined not to look over at Vinnie's table. It had been a long day, so it was time to get home and trade her shoes in for slippers. Besides Rosella wanted her guests home early.

Adeeb bid good night at the door and said he would stop by before he left in the morning. He added, "What a fun evening. I hope you will consider the offer to return. We would make a fine team."

Lila slipped into bed and thought about the buzz and stir they had caused. It would be interesting to hear the gossip at Jed's in the morning. She was sure half of it would mention this foreigner friend of Lila's. Violet would find this story quite amusing. *I must write or call tomorrow.*

In the morning, Adeeb collected his briefcase and hiking boots and thanked her for the wonderful weekend at Lilaland and added, "Rosella's B and B was first rate."

Wisely, he did not prolong the goodbye, just gave her a collaborator's hug, hopped into his Ferrari, and whisked out of the driveway. Lila phoned Violet. Violet was at a low point and did not want to talk long; therapy was leaving her weak and depressed. She said she did not want Lila to come until she was feeling better. Sadly Lila sat out in the mild warm sun, thinking about the possible loss of one of the greatest smiles to ever grace the earth. She was feeling a little melancholy, knowing that everything has its lifetime. *Even our favorite star up there, already burned through one-half of its life supply of hydro-*

gen—only five billion years to go, just a blink and a wink in the cosmic eye. Just then she looked up to see a small spider laboriously spinning a most intricate pattern between the roof overhang and the window shutter. She doesn't care that her lifetime is short, she wants to produce this work of art anyway. She was wondering if Adeeb might be right; perhaps her place was back at Brookfield, creating scientific art.

Just in time to bring her out of this slightest whiff of depression, Samuel came pedaling up the driveway and jumped off his bicycle, even before he came completely to a stop. He could not stay long as he had to run an errand for his mother in Rockton, then he had to accompany his sister to her friend's house to play. She was not to be on the road alone, you know. He wanted to know if she had purchased the supplies for the pulley system in the bee barn.

Why yes, she had, and they were still in the Jeep. He thought he might be able to help her later this week if he got his farm work done. Lila told him that would be very nice and Friday would be better than Thursday. Then he wanted to know if she had company this weekend because his father saw a fancy car in the driveway. He was happy to hear that she did because his father said that it was not right for her to be living here alone. His father seemed to think that Lila and Mr. Darthmore should consider a match. Samuel told his father that was really a bad idea because, in his opinion, they wouldn't be compatible. Lila asked Samuel how he got so wise. Samuel said that it ran in his genes.

To cap off the afternoon, Lila and Benny walked up to the bridge and enjoyed each other's company, listening to the trickle of the water and a few bird songs. Benny did not want Lila to do or be anybody but his buddy.

As the day was waning, Benny jumped up and his ears perked to half-mast. Then his head tilted slightly toward the path. Lila watched him to see what he had to say, still a little anxious considering the recent discovery of Buddy. Then Benny watched the path intently and his tail wagged, telling Lila that someone he knew was approaching. She glanced down the trail just as Vinnie came into view. Vinnie stopped and gave a hesitant hello. Lila gave back a hesitant hello.

"Is this a private party or can anyone join?"

"Not just anyone, but you are welcome."

"I was just on my way home and I thought I would stop by for a couple of minutes."

Lila decided to stay silent and did not acknowledge.

"I guess you have been busy with company."

"Yes, so true."

"Just an old friend or someone new?"

"He doesn't fall into either category."

"Well I could not help but notice that he was fawning all over you at Michael's. And you were enjoying every tender moment."

"Why, Vincent, if I did not know better, I would say you are a little jealous."

"I am just looking out for your welfare. I think Mr. Dandy Man is way out of your league."

"I will write your advice on a sticky note and keep it next to my heart as protection."

They sat silently for a few minutes, and Benny nudged in between them as if he wanted to stem some strong emotions sailing on the breeze. Lila decided to change the subject and gave Vinnie an update on Violet. He asked if she was contemplating a trip down to Gatlinburg. He mentioned that he had never been there and it might make a nice trip.

Again Lila felt the need to change the subject, so she asked him if he saw her five minutes of fame on TV. Why yes, he had, and he said that she handled herself in a most charming way, considering the questions being tossed at her. She said that she may have done better if he had shown up to help. Looking chastised, Vinnie countered that he felt that Lila deserved all the credit and his presence would have downplayed her role.

After a moment of silence, he reached over across Benny and slipped a loose strand of Lila's hair behind her ear and mentioned that he liked her new hairstyle with his hand lingering a few seconds too long down across her shoulders. Surprised with the heat of his touch, Lila sat there, thinking that it was Vinnie who was way out of her league and she had better keep her own counsel. Jealous, Benny wiggled a little closer to Lila but kept a watchful eye on Vinnie.

Now Vinnie changed the subject by saying that they could start the railing construction next week as he had a few days before starting a new job. With the sun and temperature waning, Lila stood and started for the house. Vinnie and Benny silently followed.

At the cottage door, Vinnie said, "Just don't do anything rash, that is all I am asking."

Lila answered, "I have probably done fewer rash things than 99 percent of the people walking this earth. That may be one of my biggest failings."

Vinnie, answered, "But that is what makes you unique and special.

Oh, dear special me, she thought, *there is that* special *word again. I wonder what that means in Vinnie's dictionary?*

The next morning, Caroline came rumbling up the driveway in her very muscular black pickup. It was one of those large powerful ones with dual wheels on the back; she hauled horse vans, riding paraphernalia, kids, and equipment around the country to various shows and venues. And Caroline was rather powerfully built herself in a superwoman sort of way. At the local rodeos, she was winning all the barrel races at nine years of age. Today she came ready to help install Lila's irrigation system and had already built the intake box with side screens to filter out leaves and debris which float down Alder Run. They spent several hours running the line and installing a hose system inside the garden. Lila knew that the dry season was coming soon, so it would be great to have this system up and running.

Lila tried to pay for the help but Caroline said she would rather have a few vegetables from time to time and she might need a little help at the riding academy. She remembered that Lila was handy around horses in an almost uncanny way. Lila was a little uncertain about having any special equestrian knowledge as she did not own a horse and only rode with Caroline occasionally. Caroline reminded her that Trigger would come to her when they were trying to catch him from the pasture.

Lila suggested that was only because she did not approach him with a bridle in her hand. They shared a few laughs and childhood memories of several of their riding adventures. Caroline remembered the time they thought they were lost, and Lila said that they might be but she was sure that her horse wasn't. He had been fighting her lead for the last half-hour. And sure enough, when Lila gave him his choice, he headed back to the barn with enthusiasm. Lila laughed and said that yes, if Caroline found herself shorthanded, that she would help from time to time.

Caroline did not have time to stay for lunch, but she wanted to remind Lila to set up the dinner party for their meeting with Vinnie so they might discuss buying and restoring the homestead over in Goshen. Lila said she had not forgotten, so she would call him tonight and see if he might be free on the weekend. She also told Caroline about her last phone conversation with Violet and this had her very worried.

The evening was beautiful, a perfect time to weed a few rows in the garden. There was a soft breeze blowing up from Tennessee, bringing messages from Violet that she was feeling *"better"* and not so *"nauseous."* Later at bedtime, in her nightclothes, Lila sat down to write Violet an encouraging letter. She wrote that she did try the old sewing machine, and after oiling all the little ports, it ran like a gem. She planned to sew up some surprise for Violet, for old times' sake. She described the whole scenario about Oscar apprehending Jack and ordering him to dig up his buried dog. Violet would get a laugh out of imagining Jewel's reaction to Mr. Whitey Tightie.

After signing off, she sat feeling restored and contemplating the future. Perhaps she should hike up to Caleb's very soon to contemplate what Adeeb said about returning to Brookfield Chemical but only under renewed and written promises from the board of directors which was unlikely in her estimation. Possibly she could return to Lilaland on weekends to take care of the bees and perhaps give her hens to Samuel so he could earn a little money from the egg business. "But first, I should tie up loose ends here with Mrs. Swanson, Caroline, and Marguerite. Although I may be overstating my importance in each case. All three women probably know how to trim their own sails without my advice."

Defining Moments

Lila made a note to herself to touch base with Marguerite in the morning. Jed had been a little worried since she had missed work several times, and he was also wondering how the elixir for his grandson was progressing. And Lila wanted to check on the operation of the new equipment. She went to bed reading *Cures and Prevention by Natural Medicine*. This book had some comparative literature on raki, Ayurveda, and alchemy.

After several restless hours of half-sleep, she heard Benny come into the room, snuffling and circling her bed. She reached out and patted his head and encouraged him to get back to his bunk. The second time he came in, he was surly and more insistent that there was something amiss. Lila went over to the window to check the front yard for possible raccoon or other night critters. One thing for sure, if she smelled skunk, Benny was staying inside. After several serious sniffs, she thought she caught the smell of smoke. This called for a complete inside inspection as well as a step out onto the porch and patio, with Benny on her heels, where the smell of smoke was getting slightly stronger.

Soon the Rockton fire signals started to wail, calling out the small squad of volunteer firemen. This made Lila's hair dance with prickles. She would always remember the night that her cousin's house caught on fire and he was seriously burned going back into the house to search for his daughter. Fortunately his daughter had climbed out on the roof and jumped, but her dad was in Alma Hospital for several weeks. This tragedy provoked Fire Chief Randy Davis to start an educational program on fire safety, urging families to choose a site where they agreed to meet when escaping from a burning house. Lila remembered that they provided the family housing until they got back on their feet. It was a cozy arrangement with wall-to-wall bunks and sleeping bags in the living room of their small cottage.

As the first wailing engine rumbled past her house, she thought of all her friends who lived further up that road, Vinnie, Samuel, Caroline. She looked back through the woods and saw Jack and Jewel's bedroom light snap on. Now that sleep was impossible, she decided to change out of nightclothes and pulled on the gardening clothes which she had tossed across the back of a chair. Watching from her bedroom window, she saw the fire police car and a second engine following with sirens blaring. Hurrying to the front porch, she was trying to decide whether to drive up the road to see what might be happening. She knew that Rockton had only two engines, so she would not be interfering with traffic. As she sat there, indecisive, several cars shot past, with that whirling light which they place on the roof, obviously volunteers that go straight to the fire. Soon her curiosity took over and she grabbed her barn coat, found her keys, and headed up the road.

Fortunately all was quiet at Vinnie's house, but she noticed that his lights were on. Two miles further, she could see down the lane to Samuel's place and there were no flashing lights there. Several miles further, she could see a red sky up over the next hill. Sniffing the air for the smell of smoke, she could taste the fear backing up into her throat. Someone was in trouble somewhere. *Please, please don't let it be Caroline, not Caroline.* But after several more miles, the answer was obvious—her barn was ablaze with emergency commotion everywhere: men running, shouting orders, manning hoses. She thought or imagined that she heard Caroline screaming. As she approached the scene, a fire police hailed her down and refused to let her get any closer.

Lila knew that she had passed a small gravel road which went along the back of the house, so she backed up and approached from the back. Parking her car off to the side of the house, she raced around to the front and saw Caroline dragging two frightened horses by their halters. Over the noise and flames, she shouted to Lila to take them along the fence up into the orchard. Lila grabbed for them, not knowing if she could handle two horses at once, especially not frightened horses.

She was relieved to hear Vinnie calling her; he had followed her to the fire. He chased after her and grabbed for the halters which she relinquished far too easily, feeling a little bit like a nonhero here, but she could see that the frightened horses were even a challenge for Vinnie. Coming to her senses, she shouted over the roaring inferno that Caroline wanted them to take the horses up into the orchard out of sight of the fire. Over the horrendous barn fire sounds, she half-mouthed and half-mimed that she would run back to her Jeep and fetch the rope which she had purchased for her pulley system in the bee barn.

This gave her a purpose rather than standing there, feeling a little bit of a failure at a task that Caroline could have handled with ease. Hanging onto the horses, Vinnie coaxed with all the quiet soothing words that he could remember from his much-earlier riding days. Further away from the fire, the horses did calm a bit, but they were still tossing their heads back down toward the commotion and giving Vinnie a tug of war. With the rope and a flashlight in hand, Lila raced back up along the orchard fence and found Vinnie and the horses well-hidden from the fire. She tossed the rope to him as she held the horses and talked to them in low reassuring animal noises; amazingly they started to nuzzle into her shoulder. Vinnie tied the two to each other and then to the fence.

Within minutes, he ran back down to help with horse rescue, only to meet Caroline's husband coming up with two more horses. Vinnie retrieved the two frightened horses and brought them up to the fence. Being a construction man, he pulled out a sharp pocket-knife and cut enough of the rope to tie two more horses. Lila did her best to calm all four, and the first two, which had settled, did a lot to calm this new pair. Then Vinnie met Caroline coming up the hill empty-handed and out of breath.

She said that fire had nearly reached the stables, so two firemen helped her shove and push the rest out into the corral where she opened several gates for the horses to escape out into the woods. Even so, she had to prod them out through the gates. She wanted to go back in to make sure all were out of the barn, but the fireman refused to let her back into the barn. The smoke inside was making it impossible to see and the heat was intolerable. The trio moved back down through the orchard where they could watch the disaster from a safe distance and Caroline was wondering out loud why her husband did not come back up to look for her. From their lower vantage point, they heard the fire chief command, "The barn is doomed, turn all hoses onto the house!"

At this point, Caroline felt that the house was not in much danger since it was quite a distance from the barn. She mentioned that in some colder climates, the barns are attached to the house. *Ugh, how awful*, thought Lila. No truly, Caroline said that she had read about it in *National Geographic* magazine. She was feeling secure now, believing that all the horses were safe, and she remembered that the barn and horses were well-insured; although Carl, her husband, did grumble about the premium.

But a high piercing scream, such as none of them recognized, careened though the air and seemed to carry on for several minutes. Caroline bolted upright and Lila reflexively grabbed onto her arm and Vinnie jumped up and held onto Lila. Easily slipping Lila's grasp, Caroline raced down the hill, stumbling and tripping but never truly falling. Vinnie raced down after her, but he was no match for an overly excited herculean woman.

Lila stayed back, cowardly frozen to her spot with prickles and hives, remembering her cousin's search for his daughter in an unforgiving fire. Sitting there, alone and thinking this over, she was certain that the scream was not human which was what Caroline might have been thinking. She found her flashlight on the ground and made her way back up to the tied horses. They were nickering and pawing at the ground. She did her best to soothe all four horses.

Finally Vinnie found his was back up to tell Lila that everyone was safe and accounted for. The consensus was that the scream could only have come from a horse which had been missed and left in the barn through all the excitement and chaos. He told her that Caroline had fainted, so her husband took her over to a neighbor's house and they were making her a calming tea.

Right at the edge of the orchard, Lila and Vinnie sat for a time until Carl came for the four horses. The fire was now tamed and the firemen, acting as though everything was under control, were strutting with a job well done. Amen and amen! Together they led the horses back to the riding school corral which was far enough away from the barn to escape damage. Lila told Carl that she would come back tomorrow to help round up the other horses. Now it was nearly 4:00 a.m.

Vinnie followed Lila home and walked her to the door. Lila was shivering prickles with after-fright and a letdown depression. As she put her hand on the doorknob, he pulled her back gently into his chest, trying to calm the shaking. She succumbed to the comforting embrace for the moment. After all, if wonder woman Caroline could faint, she could allow herself a weak moment. Vinnie sniffed her hair and said that he always liked the aroma of burning barn shampoo which made Lila snuffle and swallow the fear which was still wallowing in her throat.

"You had better get home for several hours of sleep before work. You usually start at 6:00 a.m."

"I would not be able to sleep now."

"Well, at least get your shower and a little breakfast before work."

"I have a better idea."

"Which is?"

"Why don't I come in and make you an omelet while you get a hot shower?"

"I am not sure about that."

"What? Chicken lady has no eggs in the house? I am quite skilled in the kitchen. After all, I design and build them."

Lila went for a shower, and Vinnie yelled, "Take your time, I need a little space now."

The hot water, combined with soothing lavender soap, did wonders for the shivers. She let the steamy rivulets of water wash away some of the angst and pain of memory. After several luxurious minutes, however, she started to think of Caroline and wondered if Carl or the neighbor was helping her through these frightfully difficult moments. It will take years for her to erase the sound of a horse meeting his hell on earth. Lila knew that Caroline would wake up from bad dreams for a long time.

She took her time toweling and drying her hair. She was never into makeup, but she found a little color for her face. Lila took her time looking in the mirror, and she realized, for the first time, that aging lines were creeping from the corner of her mouth up past the nose; her laugh lines were having a meeting with her crow's feet and that her forehead had some new creases. She had been too busy to notice. What had she ever accomplished, she wondered? Middle age and nothing to show for it. That whiff of depression again. She smelled the aroma of Eight o'clock wafting up the stairs and that brought her back to reality.

The little kitchen table was set with her everyday china, but he found a clean tablecloth from the dining room. Always the gentleman, he pulled out her chair. Breakfast of omelet, toast, and coffee was a 10. They tried to steer conversation away from the fire, but it pushed its ugly stench into the ether, not to be put aside without a fight. They caved to its whim and let the sights and sounds win them over.

Lila was distraught for Caroline, but Vinnie reminded her how resilient she was. Lila knew that the loss was far greater than just one horse. But there was one upside; Caroline would have to move on the decision about buying Violet's homestead. They considered all the potential that could be realized there for her riding academy.

Noticing that the time was flying and that Vinnie, even now a little late, had to get to work, Lila scooped up the dirty dishes and started the sudsy water in the sink. Vinnie walked over and held her by the shoulders which sent heat and alarm bells through the atmosphere. She held tight to the hot-and-cold-water faucets. He slid his hands down her arms and covered her soapy hands. She gripped the faucets. He nuzzled her neck and said that this conversation was not finished. With a quiet firm voice, he said he was coming back tomorrow night around seven o'clock so they could reach some agreement. He would bring takeout for supper, and she should chill the wine. He turned and walked out the door, making Lila breathe a sigh of relief and dismay at the same time. As the door closure swooshed shut, she felt his loss, but she knew it was better to stop this nonsense now rather than be heartbroken later.

Before driving over to Caroline's to help with horse roundup, she and Benny left the chickens out of the coop for the day and went up to check on the bee barn. As Lila drove up to Caroline's, there was an eerie stillness with the aftermath of smoke and a stench of burned rubber, burned hay, and possibly horseflesh. She stopped at the house and a helpful neighbor said they had already gone to round up the horses. Samuel and his father had come to help. Lila walked out to the corral and found two horses standing by the corral, so she opened the gate and prodded them inside with the four others. She wanted to tell Caroline that now six were accounted for and she was not sure how many in all they were looking for. For a few minutes, she searched up through the orchard but found no one.

At the edge of the orchard, she sat down on the grass, nearly in the spot from which they had watched the fire last night. Regarding the view from up here, she saw the devastation that unforgiving fire causes. There wasn't much left but soot and few burned-out timbers. Like a sentinel standing guard, the silo was still straight and true, and the back foundation stones were holding up a little evidence of what used to be there. Several small smoke signals were slowly spiraling up out of the ashes and occasionally talked to each other as they broke into small erratic flames. The tractor shed, too close to the barn, was also destroyed, taking as its prey, the John Deere, now scorched and lacking the signature colors; the hulk of steel still remained with its burned rubber tires, causing the stench of the barn fire, more so than the consumed timber and hay. It would take a month of winds and rain to remove that smell; the saturated olfactory nerves would give up and stop smelling it long before nature finally dispensed with the particles.

But now that the barn and sheds were gone, it occurred to Lila that the landscape here really wasn't the best place for a horse ranch. It was hemmed in by other properties across the road and there wasn't much level land on this side. Just as behind Lila's place, the land started to edge upward toward the orchards and Alder Run. If Caroline hoped to expand her riding school and add training rings and corrals, Violet's homestead in Goshen was so much better suited.

And being closer to Alma, with a larger population to draw from, would not hurt either.

Since she had scheduled to meet with Marguerite this morning, she headed on down to Jed's Café. The place was buzzing with gossip about the fire. Lila did not stop and went directly to the back. Jed brought coffee back to her. Marguerite smiled a rare smile when she walked in. They set to work without saying a word; they had a peeling symphony. It was comforting to be there with Mar. In her company, Lila felt a real kinship of mind and spirit, back through the centuries. With the last potato peeled, Marguerite scraped the peels into the compost bin and washed their knives and pans. Lila sat back and watched her efficient use of motion, and Mar always seemed to be in the moment. A lesson Lila should learn. Lila's mind was often solving a secondary problem while still working on the present one. Finally Marguerite sat back down and pulled her stool close with their knees almost touching.

"Lila, I have some good news to share."

"I could use some good news right now."

"Yes, it shows on your face, right down to your toes."

"Well, I don't personally own the problems."

"Is it about Violet?"

"Yes, also Caroline, Mrs. Swanson, and others."

"Life will solve the problems while you stew and fret."

"So I have to learn how to step out of the way."

"Yes, Lila. Put your energies where you naturally excel."

"Mar, please forgive me. I am eager to hear your good news."

"My distillations and condensations have been really exceptional. I am ready to package the combined tonic, elixir, and essential oil for Jed's grandson."

"That is wonderful news. Does Jed know?"

"Yes, I told him this morning."

In celebration, Lila wanted to reach out and touch Marguerite but did not dare be so bold. She sensed that Marguerite's personal space was very close to being breached with this little knee-to-knee intimacy that she was allowing.

Instead, she said, "Mar, a friend of mine is suffering with arthritis but does not want the strong meds."

"Yes, many of my clients don't like the side effects of prescribed medicine."

"In the past, you mentioned the use of Boswellia to reduce inflammation."

"I redistill the Boswellia from India to take out all the additives and combine it with ginger and turmeric. Curcumin is the active ingredient in turmeric which needs a little black pepper to make it pass the gut."

"Bioavailability, as we say in the business. Would ingesting it with a meal be best?"

"Yes, that is the recommendation. In my experience, treatment with Boswellia only works if the arthritis is treated early before all the cartilages are destroyed."

"I think that my friend's condition has only just begun, so this may help him."

"I will bring you one month's treatment, free of charge, for him to try."

"Mar, that would be overly generous of you."

As Lila drove home, she was thinking about how to prepare for Vinnie's visit and she was anxious to tell him about Marguerite's medical elixir for arthritis. She stopped at her mailbox and found the usual ads and advertisements, but just at the bottom, she found an official letter from Brookfield Chemical with the fancy blue letterhead. She knew they were in a cost cutting round, and she suspected this was the ax to her agreement.

Just then, Samuel was pedaling down the road with real gusto, so she stopped to see if he was coming to visit. Yes, his father gave him some time off to help her with the pulley system up in the bee barn. She told Samuel that she only needed five minutes to change into barn clothes and then she would meet him at the barn. The Brookfield bad-news letter could wait for a quieter time.

Up in the barn, Samuel had already studied the rope which had been cut last night for the horses. He measured it out and figured that there was still ample for the project. He had the pulleys set out along the measured lengths when she arrived. Her heart swelled with admiration as she watched his serious intent face. How lucky she was to have this young man for a friend. Someday some charming young lady would steal his heart. Lila did not dwell on the fact that she did not have children, but right here, right now, she envied Samuel's parents. What generous people they are to share him.

They calculated and recalculated before cutting and installing the pulley system. Lila had to run down to the house to bring up the stepladder to help with the installation. Her natural cost cutting measures of sharing one stepladder between the house and bee barn were starting to irritate her. With the stepladder in place, they were able to slide several more boards over onto the rafters that were safe enough to step out onto while installing the hooks and ropes. From Lila's vantage point above, she looked down at Samuel who seemed to be in a mesmerized state with his eyes rolling in a circular pattern, following a bee who was traveling back and forth on the brim of his hat.

"I think he wants to buy my hat." He chuckled.

"No." Lila said that she was pretty sure that this particular bee would need a bonnet instead, like Rebekah wears. She explained that guard honeybees were female, and besides, this bee was not big enough to be a drone. She decided to forestall any further conversation of what the drone's purpose in the hive amounted to, even though this intelligent farm boy would have already worked out all of nature's dynamics between the male and female honeybee species. But after all, this was not her son!

Samuel's father donated an old canvas cover which she could use for the sling basket; they attached it to the rope with hook-and-eye hardware. Once they were finished, Samuel hauled the basket up to the loft and told Lila to put several bee frames into the sling which he proudly lowered to the barn floor. And just as proudly, he hauled the load back up to Lila. They celebrated with high fives. Samuel had to hurry back home to his own farm work. For his mother, she wrapped up a jar of honey and some purified beeswax for candles or furniture polish.

Now it was time to open the bad newsletter, only to be flummoxed with an offer that she would have to consider. The current head of the regional Brookfield Plant was offering her the position of supervisor in the immunotherapy department with a large office and technical support. He apologized for the past mistakes which some of his colleagues (unnamed) made when assessing her worth to the future progress at Brookfield. When they allowed her to step down without a counteroffer, they did not call in any of the technicians which she had trained. But now, with the insistence of several current highly regarded researchers, they have consulted many who would like to see her back in the role of supervisor. Unfortunately the good news was tainted a little by adding, "Salary to be negotiated," with the unfortunate caveat added in the post script that Brookfield was in the process of cost cutting, so the salary may not be as they would wish to offer just now, but that issue would be revisited in the next year's budget.

Digesting the letter, Lila substituted "Adeeb Guyesudin" for "highly regarded researchers," and it did not take long to realize Adeeb's earnest wish to have her back as a collaborator. Lila was worried that it might have been just a whim of his that would pass. *Well, if they think I would come back at the old salary level, they are sorely mistaken. But then again, maybe I should give them a chance to explain their offer.*

The phone jangled her back to reality. It was Vinnie, apologizing that he could not keep his date tonight. Would tomorrow night work for her? She was surprised, disappointed, and relieved, all in that order; after a brief pause, she told him that tomorrow night would be much better for a variety of reasons and especially since she needed to get to bed early anyway.

"Quite frankly, I am exhausted." Smiling to herself, she heard Buster's Bar noises in the background and a woman's voice, asking "Vinnie, are you coming?"

Lila put down the phone and was thinking, *Yes, Vinnie is way, way beyond my league. Anyone yearning for Vinnie's undivided affections would always be disappointed.*

The next morning's fog cleared with a sunshine, interrupted with tumbling clouds, eager to get Lila's feet on the ground. A good night sleep put her on solid footing. She poured coffee into a thermos and packed up several hard-boiled eggs. After letting the hens out for the day, she donned some hiking gear and headed out; she needed to hike up to Caleb's. From up there, she could sort out the thoughts that were competing for her attention. As always, Benny was eager to get started.

She sat down on the familiar smooth stone, where Caleb must have sat many years ago, and let the past few weeks drift over her—all of it, the good and the bad. The sun was peeking in and out, so she took off her jacket and let the sun and clouds dance on her face and forearms. The particles in the ether were tousling her hair, prickling her scalp. Benny came back from foraging and sat down, putting pressure on her boot to let her know that whatever happened, he wanted to be part of the decision.

Attempting to see her future, she decided to let the cards fall into place rather than forcing an inside straight. Marguerite's sage advice came back to her in whispered clarity, "You must stop fussing over the little things and put your energies where you excel!"

Taking that advice would mean that I should set up an appointment at Brookfield to discuss coming back into the laboratory with negotiated time off to come back for honey harvest. Number 2: I must go down to Gatlinburg to see Violet and take her the bed jacket sewn on the beloved Singer sewing machine (Jewel helped her finish the project and added a few sequins). Number 3: I will confer with Marguerite to see if we can make plans for a collaboration on the honey skin cream. Number 4: Stop worrying about Mrs. Swanson and the university retreat, those gears have already been set in motion. Number 5: Caroline, well, Caroline can take care of all matters at Violet's homestead quite well on her own, thank you very much. She already has most of the furniture, and who knows, she may even have the commode. Number 6: I must see if Samuel can take the hens, including George. And will Jack and Jewel look in on the cottage from time to time?

And of course, there is Vinnie. We still need to clear the air. I want very much to remain good neighbors and bartering friends. Vinnie will go on being Vinnie.

"And yes, Benny, wherever we go, we go together!"

About the Author

The author, Sarah Johnston, is a native of Central Pennsylvania but now resides in Upstate New York, with her husband, Daniel, and their cat, Chester. In this beautiful Finger Lakes region, they raised two young men, Brendan and Scott, who bring joy into their lives.

Sarah is now retired from a long career in academia and biomedical research, having obtained degrees from Penn State, University of Buffalo, and the University of Rochester. Her research career emphasis was in immunochemistry and autoimmune diseases, and when time allowed, she gardened and kept honeybees. Growing up in a household where most medical issues were successfully solved at home, she has maintained a lifelong interest in alternative and folklore medicine. After retiring from research, Sarah and her husband have immersed themselves into community-enrichment programs.